SCIENCE! Of the Lambs

Chris Koehler

ISBN-978-0-9987323-3-6

Cover design by: Ezra Rendleman

Library of Congress Control Number: 2024922467

Printed in the United States of America

Acknowledgment

I would like to thank my mother for editing and proofreading this so many times.

My friends at the Carolina Forest Authors club for their help and advice.

Ezra Rendelmen for the cover.

And you for reading this.

I also want to blame Richard (you know who you are) for making a pun so bad I had to write a book around it.

CHAPTER 1

My alarm went off for the fifth time; it was nearly 8:00 am, and I had to get up to make it to work on time. So naturally, I hit snooze one more time before getting up at the sixth alarm. I then did everything I needed to; I put on some clothes, a T-shirt, and I put on some blue jeans. I would have worn shorts but you can't wear shorts in a lab.

My name is Trixie Night… please stop laughing, I know my name is funny. Anyway, I was working at a lab run by my advisor Dr. Calamity. She was doing some weird stuff with genetics, cutting edge, but odd. She was good though, but the other lab assistant was… well… you'll see.

My rental house had four bedrooms, each with its own bathroom, and connected to a shared common area with a kitchen via a hallway. I was at the far end, away from the kitchen and the front door. Normally we had four people living here, but for now, two were away on summer vacation, and the only one other than me was in the process of being kicked out. The rest of us caught her stealing food and the rental company agreed to get rid of her. Apparently, she was about three months behind on rent anyway.

Breakfast was my usual, two cups of coffee, with lots of cream, and a bowl of cereal. Then it was off to the lab via my car, Hank.

Hank was an old beat-up thing that my parents handed down to me when I went off to college. He was old then, and he is older now. But he's one of those Japanese cars that seemed determined to outlive the sun. Dented bumpers and scratched paint covered his outside. The inside was still nice-ish, the seats even looked good, almost new. Getting in and hearing the engine crank for one second too long, the uninitiated might think that Hank had finally given up the ghost. But Hank was stubborn, not ready to go yet, reliable, and like always, just needed a second to warm up before revving up.

Then it was off to the labs where I was working for the summer. I spent a moment wondering, like I did every morning, if perhaps it had been a mistake to go to college so far from home, but the Dedlam University of Montana, or D.U.M., as way too many snarky freshmen called it, was a good university. Well… not really, but it was the one to offer me the most scholarship money, and it had a halfway decent program. So, there's that at least.

Dedlam was not a busy place, especially in summer, when about half of the population went home. So the roads were clear, and many of the restaurants were closed or operating at reduced capacity. My usual route was being rebuilt from the ground up, so for this week, I was taking a detour. Dedlam was not the middle of nowhere, that was just five miles down the road, and the only thing it had was an okay-ish university.

I had gotten a summer job/paying internship from Dr. Calamity. There wasn't much else available. She wasn't a bad teacher, but I still hated working for her over the summer. It mostly wasn't her fault, though her work got a little weird. She specialized in genetics and was smart enough to be a leader in her field, but she chose Dedlam. I don't know why. Presumably, they offered more money, or more freedom or something. Still, the lab itself was not the best.

I got to the lab a few minutes early. Got inside, and as per usual, Jay took the opportunity to stare directly at my breasts with all the subtlety of a thunderstorm.

"Mr. Walker. Leave her alone," said Dr. Calamity.

"I wasn't…" protested Jay.

"I could see you do it, Walker," said Dr. Calamity. "Now leave Trixie alone or I will talk to H.R… again."

Jay rolled his eyes, because we didn't have half an H.R, aside from Dr. Calamity. Neither of us liked him, his work was sloppy and subpar, and I didn't know why he was still here. If it were cooler, I would have worn a baggy sweater to cover my assets, but it was summer, and the university's lab did not have air conditioning. For now, so early in the morning, that was not an issue. But give it time.

Dr. Calamity spent most of the day in her office but kept the door open so she could come when we needed her to. She was young for a professor, blond, and had various mad scientist posters plastered on her office wall, along with one poster dedicated to beer. She dressed casually, though lab-appropriate, long pants and close-toed shoes. Both of which were a drag in the hot summer in a lab run by a university that shunned A.C. Not like any of the regular, not here for the summer, students needed it anyway, right?

Anyway Jay, or Mr. Walker as Dr. Calamity called him, was deviously handsome; that was the complete list of his positive qualities. His personality was like the north end of a southbound goat. On a good day, he was a sleaze-ball, the kind of boy that all but the most relaxed, almost negligent, fathers would have nightmares about their daughters bringing home, or even interacting with in any way but to avoid. He could be charitably described as lazy, refused to remember things we told him five seconds ago, and spent more time applying hair gel than anything else.

The lab itself had a lab fridge in the back, which was an ordinary kitchen fridge and freezer. The counters were stained with decades of spills by many freshmen at what many considered a party school. The corner had a sink, eyewash station, and gloves/masks/goggles/ other safety stuff. The counters were cultured with various forms of lab equipment, beakers, burners, microscopes, and the walls were dingy. Calamity's office was next to the main lab and near the break room. This contained the food-safe fridge, which was a mini-fridge, and a TV mounted on the wall. This day, as on many days, the lab stank of formaldehyde and preservatives. A constant buzz emanated from a dozen fans set up to provide some relief from the heat we would be feeling later in the day.

I put my lunch in the break fridge, and I got onto my duties, far away from Jay. No doubt he would screw something up later and Dr. Calamity would be busy and I would have to come over and he would take the opportunity to leer at me again. If I was lucky, I wouldn't have to do half of his work for him.

Dr. Calamity came by to speak with me.

"So for today, I want you to focus on some dissections," said Calamity. "Specifically of some frogs I am about to kill, your job will be to look for any anomalies."

"By any chance were these frogs previously rats yesterday morning?" I asked.

"Well, maybe… yeah."

"Then I have found one anomaly."

"Just keep an eye out for anything that shouldn't be there in a frog. I will get you the first one in a few minutes so you should go set up. I have a total of five frogs for you to dissect, take any notes you need to, and photograph any anomalies. Let me know when you are done with the first one and I will get you the second."

"Right." I got to my station and got it ready for the first frog. Once Dr. Calamity delivered it, I got to work. It should have taken an hour, but Jay kept pestering me about some questions with an answer that should have been obvious. Such as, no we don't have AC here, yes you should ask Dr. Calamity where that goes, I don't recognize it, yes the test tubes need to be dried and go on the test tube drying rack, no we don't have a dishwasher for that, and many other pointless questions that he asked every day. At almost every encounter I could feel his eyes undressing me. And he tried several times to get me to "Go on a date" with him. Something I might have considered had he been actually nice, not just pretending to be nice in the hopes of getting laid.

Three hours went by and I had only dissected two frogs, the growing heat of the lab meant that my protective gloves became rather uncomfortable and sweaty. And the smell was no doubt made worse by the 80-degree F heat. It was time for lunch and I saw Jay cleaning something up in the fridge. It was a lab vial containing a spilled, clear blue, solution, it was supposed to be a food-safe fridge.

"Jay, what did you spill in the fridge?" I asked.

"Ummm… A soda?" he said.

"I can see the sideways beaker… in the food-safe fridge!"

That got Dr. Calamity's attention, she stood up and came over from her office.

"No… it's just soda I swear."

"NO, IT'S NOT!!!" said Dr. Calamity, seeing what was spilled. "That solution, one, it should never be in a food-safe fridge because it is a bit of a biohazard, and two, DO YOU HAVE THE SLIGHTEST IDEA HOW MUCH IT COST???????"

"But… You said to put it in the fridge," said Jay.

"Mr. Walker… I told you to put it in the lab fridge, not the break room fridge… I didn't think I needed to specify that the first time, but since then I have learned. It is clear to me that you haven't… may I direct your attention to the screen."

Dr. Calamity pulled out a remote and turned on a TV in the break room. Then started playing a recording, of herself.

"Hello, Mr. Walker," began the recording. "If you are seeing this message, then you have screwed up again, and as such, in a few short moments, you will be fired."

Jay turned to the real Dr. Calamity. "You can't do that," he said. "My father is the dean of this school."

"Oh, but I can do that," continued the recording just after a now wide-eyed Jay tried to tell off a now rather smug Dr. Calamity. "You see, you have screwed up many times, I have recordings of much of this on camera, and while your father protected you, the school board has heard what I have been telling them, and they decided that I was to give you a final warning, and if you screwed up again after that, I was to fire you, and if your father complains, he can also be fired." The recorded Dr. Calamity held up a piece of paper, "I have this in writing by the way."

Suddenly the recording switched to one of Jay and Dr. Calamity talking.

"You received that warning, and as such if you caused problems again by stealing Trixie's lunch again, or molesting her again, or stealing my lunch again, or by what I am guessing happened here, you violated a lab safety protocol again, probably putting lab supplies in the food-safe office fridge. I absolutely can and will fire you, and now that has come to pass."

"You must have a dozen of these," said Jay to the real Dr. Calamity.

"No just one," said the recording. causing Jay to turn to the screen with wide eyes.

The recording continued, "Now future me will be giving you half an hour to grab your stuff and get out of my lab before she calls security."

The recording finished.

"Well, you heard past me," said Dr. Calamity with eerie tranquility before giving a mocking smile. "Best of luck on your future endeavors, you'll need it."

Jay, now sweating more than the heat alone made necessary, left shortly thereafter. Dr. Calamity sighed and examined the fridge.

"So much for that solution, damn that's going to be a setback, looks like it was contained, I don't see anything near your lunchbox. Should be fine."

"I will let you know if it tastes funny," I said.

My food didn't taste funny. I didn't notice anything off until an hour after my lunch when I had trouble with the tools for the next dissection, then when changing gloves, I saw that my fingers had… changed. Somehow the nails became more like blunt hammers across the entire end of the finger. I was also much warmer, and I saw white hairs all over my arm.

"Dr. Calamity," I said, "I think something is wrong with me."

"Does something hurt, feel funny?" she said coming out of her office, then she saw my changing hands, and her jaw dropped.

"No no no no no no. This… oh my, what happened, was it… when did you notice?"

"Just a few minutes ago… my voice… what happened to my voice."

"I am so sorry," began Calamity. "The solution that Mr. Walker spilled… it was… similar to the one that I gave the rats yesterday."

"So I'm turning into a rat?" I asked, feeling rather alarmed.

"Well… the solution was to turn an animal… into a sheep."

"Is that meant to be comforting?"

"Um… no just the truth… listen I have a plan to… fix this… but I have to let the change run through its course first. But I can reverse it… you… did you see… this is an important question because those frogs that became rats, were originally frogs… did you see anything odd about them."

"NO. WHAT DOES THAT HAVE TO DO WITH ANYTHING?"

"Because now I know I can fully reverse it… and now just try to stay calm. I will fix this I promise. Just come with me."

Dr. Calamity led me to a back room of the labs. I noticed that walking felt weird, I kept having to balance on tables and walls. She rapidly cleared out the room, I failed to recognize some of the equipment. I felt weak, and I started to cry.

"Ok," said Dr. Calamity after she finished clearing out the room. "You will stay here, I will make the cure… it will take me some time to do that… so try to stay calm, remember… I will fix this. But I will have to work in the lab… I'm sorry but I can't be here for you."

"Ok… go," I said, between tears. Dr. Calamity ran off.

I didn't see her for a while after that. My vision began changing; green, red, and yellow all looked the same. After an hour… two… I couldn't tell time, I leaned on the wall to look out the window, and the grass outside began to look tasty. I then began to wonder if eating grass and being Dr. Calamity's pet sheep would be the worst thing in the world. But my parents… who are my parents… I can't remember their faces anymore; I can't remember Dr. Calamity's face… or anyone's. I tried to yell for Dr. Calamity, but a baaa came out. Things began to feel weird, unpleasant, and sometimes painful, after that my memory began to become foggy, I don't remember anything after that point.

CHAPTER 2

My next memory is waking up as a human. My first reaction was that turning into a sheep was a bad dream, then my stomach compelled me to find a toilet or a trash can as it was going to empty itself and whatever was in there would come right back out the way it came in. Luckily an unoccupied bathroom was nearby so I was able to empty my stomach into a toilet with relative ease.

"Easy there, tiger," said a familiar voice behind me. "You looked really baaad when my wife brought you in yesterday, take it easy."

After I was confident that my stomach was empty, I looked up and saw my English professor at Dedlam. He was tall, looked to be about the same age as Dr. Calamity, probably not even thirty. Also, he was handsome enough that you could imagine a female student would deliberately flunk his class. Just so that she could offer to do "anything" to make up her grade.

"Dr. Deer?" I exclaimed. "I… What happened? Did… How?"

"Ama brought you here yesterday evening, said you had gotten hurt in her lab. Wanted to keep you for the night to make sure you were OK. Also please call me John, and my wife Ama, we aren't being your professors right now."

"Right… John did Dr. Calami-… Ama tell you what happened?"

"She gave me the short version. I have nothing going on today so she asked me to take care of you until she got back, said she had some stuff she needed to do at the lab."

"Ok… Thanks."

I took a look at what were the contents of my stomach, they were very green, and I think I saw some grass in there.

"Do you remember what happened?" asked Dr. Dee- erm, John. "Ama said you might not."

"It's complicated and… I don't want to talk about it," I said. "Maybe later, but I can remember… some of it."

"Sounds fair," said John. "I will call Ama, and let her know you're up, if you need anything let me know, I will be doing some work for the university, but it's not too urgent so don't hesitate to ask me for something."

I nodded, while wondering if there was anything else that was going to come up from my stomach. After waiting a minute to ensure that there wasn't, I flushed it all down and tried to rest on the couch. On the way over I realized that every muscle in my body was sore. After getting to the couch, I realized I didn't have my purse with me. I recalled that was because the pants I had on at the time were men's pants, and thus had pockets, and furthermore, I was still wearing them. After checking my pockets, I found to my relief that I had everything.

I took a moment to register that if John had the short version, then he might know what happened. I thought about asking him… but decided that I would rather not. He might tell me something I would rather not know… or I might let information out that he shouldn't hear. So I rested on the couch.

I checked my phone, discovered that Dr… Ama must have recharged it for me, and that it was Friday… it was Thursday when I went to the lab to be turned into a sheep. Meaning that I missed the season finale of my favorite show… damn. Mom is going to be all about that on Twitface. UGGGGG.

I checked my email, lots of spam, and one message from the university board telling me that they were sorry about my injury and hoped I wouldn't sue them. Literally, they said, "Sorry, please don't sue." I also got one rather unhinged-sounding thing from Jay's father ranting about how I "Got him fired" and "Got my Son fired", how I was a "Stupid Witch" and how "The only good thing you have is those huge knockers." It would have been funny had he not threatened to "pound your witch holes until you croak" but that was it for the email.

So I tried to rest; checked my webcomics for today and yesterday. I checked Twitface, watched some stupid internet videos, and tried to figure out what to say to mom and dad about this, or if to say anything at all. While it was the first time I have been turned into a sheep I had been already been threatened by some idiot who would "Pound your Witch Holes until I croak." Which is why I don't talk to Uncle Ed anymore. And also why mom and dad insisted I take some self-defense classes. Though thanks to Jay's father's threats, I would have to watch myself. Make sure I am always on a security camera, near people, in well-lit parking lots, watching strangers, and watching my drink at restaurants and bars. I would have to be wary of Jay or his father appearing from any dark place, and looking for an attacker who could come from anywhere or be any man. In other words, business as usual.

Dr. Calamity came back late afternoon.

"Are you feeling better?" she asked.

"Well… yes," I said, not sure what other answer she expected.

"Good," said Dr. Calamity. "Come into my office we can talk privately."

I followed her upstairs and sat down across from her.

Once we sat down I said, "First Question, why do you have a drink that turns people into sheep?

"It is the work I find most interesting," said Calamity.

I must have looked at her like she had three heads.

She smiled, "If you wanted to know why I wanted to do this work… if we can turn a person into a sheep, we could turn a person with cancer into a person without cancer."

I alternated between nodding and shaking my head "I understand, but also don't."

"What parts do you and do you not understand?"

"I understand wanting to cure cancer, I am not sure how turning a person into a sheep helps."

She shrugged, "I have been around this stuff so long I forget how weird it sounds. Anyway, if I can make a treatment that can turn every cell of your body into a sheep's cell, and rearrange it quickly into an actual sheep's body, I can turn every cancerous cell in a body into a healthy cell, and rearrange the tumor into healthy tissue."

"I guess that makes sense," I said.

"We also get inquiries about diabetes, amputees, other disabilities like blindness and deafness, cosmetic surgeons, and transgender health advocates," said Calamity.

I pondered for a moment, "I can see that. I guess it makes sense. What we are doing now is just the groundwork."

"This could be the biggest medical invention since vaccines and antibiotics," said Calamity. "It's the sort of thing that gets your name in history books and looks really good on a resume."

I nodded, "Anyway, about what happened to me, what is our story?" I asked, "No one is going to believe it."

"Well, the board knows the truth," began Calamity.

"UHHHHHHHHhhhhhhh…." was the only thing I could think to reply.

"I have to tell them what is going on in my lab for reasons of safety, security, ethics, budget, and for various legal reasons," said Calamity. "That is just how it works; they knew about the experiments going on here. When an accident happens, they need to know what happened, why it happened, and what the consequences are."

Her tone shifted, she took a sharp breath, and sighed, "Though I did get the feeling that some of them weren't paying attention."

"Right," I said, "But what about…"

Calamity held her hand up, "There are privacy laws as well, what happened yesterday won't go beyond the board and the two of us. Not unless you want it to, if it makes you feel better, they are now a lot more committed to firing the dean and his son. The news on that should be going out on Monday."

"Ok… what should I do?" I ask.

"Well, I would consider suing the school," said Calamity.

"…Seriously?" I began.

"This was not the first time Mr. Walker screwed up in a way that could have hurt you," began Calamity. "I wanted to fire him so long ago for so many reasons. But the dean kept blocking me and the board protected him for far too long. You have a serious case if you go up against them in court. They ignored a dangerous employee for far too long. Also, look at this."

She then showed me an email on her phone, it looked suspiciously like the one that Walker Senior sent me.

"I got one too," I said.

"Which is good evidence against them," said Calamity. "Also if you take legal action you could one, get a nice payout for yourself, two, send them the message that they should have done this a long time ago, and three, get this guy on a watch list so that he doesn't hurt anyone. And four, all of that would maybe force the board to undergo surgery to remove their head from their butts."

"Right," I said now genuinely considering that.

"If you need a lawyer, I know a very good one." She handed me the business card of a law firm called "Sue Em, & Quick."

"Are you serious?" I asked.

"Yep," said Calamity, "I have a good excuse, that I tried to get rid of Mr. Walker earlier. I have the paperwork to show it. I have the orders, from the dean, in writing, to rescind his firing. I have the reason why he was originally fired written down, for doing basically the same thing that eventually got you hurt. I spoke with Sue, err, Ms. Em, and she assured me that any argument that I screwed up, is cleared by the fact that the solution never should have been there in the first place. And given Mr. Walker's repeated screw-ups in the manner..." Calamity smiled, "The system doesn't always work the way it should... but when it does, ohh, it does."

"Right," I said not sure if I really wanted to go through with this, and wondering how Calamity lost her eloquence. "I will think about this."

"I would, heck I actually am," said Calamity. "You would just be joining my case."

I nodded, "Can we talk about something else?" I asked.

"Yeah, about what? Are you feeling, OK? Mentally physically?"

"I think I'm fine."

"Good, I will take you home after dinner."

"I don't think I'm hungry."

"We have pizza."

"Ok, maybe there is something wrong with me because that doesn't sound appetizing, and I haven't had lunch." I looked down, "Perhaps I am not quite well."

"With the rats… they did lose their appetite," said Calamity. "They were hungry the day after though. Maybe you should stay the night?"

"I will think about it," I said while thinking. 'Yes please, my student rental house is currently having its kitchen remastered for the fourth week of a two-week project.'

I was able to eat a slice of pizza and keep it down, which I had worried about for a moment. I settled on the couch again, wearing a spare set of PJs from Dr. Calamity that was a bit loose on me, but they were clean. The next day, after a big breakfast, Dr. Calamity drove me to the lab, and I drove Hank home.

I had all day Saturday to chill and recover like my appetite had. I also had time to decide that there was no way I would be suing as I didn't have the time for that.

CHAPTER 3

I don't know how I got talked into this, even with Calamity giving me the day off, but I got to the law office of Sue Em and Quick just before lunch. I was speaking with Ms. Em who was the lawyer Calamity wanted me to talk to.

"First, call me Sue," she said. "Second I will need you to be perfectly honest, tell me the truth, the whole truth, and nothing but the truth. I will need to know everything good, and bad, that might be even tangentially related to what happened, we clear?"

"Yes," I said hoping that personal details wouldn't come up.

Sue smiled and shifted her seat, she appeared middle-aged, 40 max, though the sign on the front door suggested that she founded the business nearly 40 years ago. Her office was decorated with various posters. My favorites included, "Everyone brings happiness to this room, some when they enter, others when they leave." One just under a picture of a young girl saying "I smile because I am your grandma, I laugh because there is nothing you can do about it." And my favorite of the bunch: "Lawyers were created so that used car salesmen could look down upon something."

"So," began Sue, "Walk me through what happened last Wednesday from your perspective."

"I got to the lab," I began. "When it was lunchtime, I noticed that Jay… Mr. Walker was cleaning up a spill in the office fridge."

"The one that was supposed to be food safe?" asked Sue.

"Yes," I said, "He had spilled a non-food solution in there. Calamity fired him on the spot for this and earlier offenses, and we tried to finish cleaning it up."

"And some of that solution got on your food?"

"Yes, and we didn't notice, until after I had eaten it."

"By which point you had sustained your 'injury" and were well on your way to becoming the supplier for my next knitting project."

I blinked a few times, "Yes."

"So just what Ama told me then… and do you recall her trying to discipline Jay previously?"

"She tried to fire him two weeks into his job. I think that she might have yelled at him about something every day he showed up to work."

"Can you recall what he was typically accused of?"

"Stealing food, putting food in the not-food-safe lab fridge, putting nonfood-safe lab equipment in the office fridge, showing up late, leering at me, putting supplies in places they did not belong, attempting to grope me once, breaking the toilet in a temper tantrum, and throwing used rat bedding all over the place, and onto me when I said no to going out on a date with him."

"And Calamity tried to discipline him after each incident," said Sue, jotting something down on a piece of paper. "She gave me records and quite a large security feed to show this. You should have lawyered up sooner, but we can still make sure he receives justice, and his father, and possibly the university board of directors." She smiled, "We are going to make this right believe me."

I nodded.

"Before I let you ask questions, I have one more," said Sue. "Have you noticed any side effects of this transformation?"

"More leg hair, and salads taste better. How long will this take though? I hear these cases can last years," I asked.

"It will probably take years," said Sue. "The price of accurate justice is slow justice."

I nodded.

"But," said Sue. "If you are willing to stay on board with me, we will get through this. I know Dr. Calamity. I sued on her behalf before, when an agricultural firm tried to steal a patent to a genetic sequence she discovered." Sue smiled, "We settled, but they were set back a few years; Calamity came out ahead."

I nodded, "I hear this can be stressful."

"It will be," said Sue. "But nowhere near as stressful as it will be for them. If they are smart, they will settle, and give us everything we want, before a judge notices."

"Ok, I will need time to think about this," I said, wondering if I might actually say yes.

"Calamity has already asked me to file," said Sue. "So you would be joining her case if you do. Go ahead and sleep on it if you need to. Just let me know as soon as you make a decision."

"Is that everything?" I asked.

"Just one more thing, then you can go," said Sue, with an evil smile, "Do you know the difference between a dead lawyer in the road and a dead skunk in the road?"

"No," I said genuinely confused.

Sue smiled, "There are skid marks before the skunk."

I texted Calamity when I was done and told her I would think about it, she responded "Good, see you tomorrow!" So I went home to relax for the day.

When I got to the lab the next day, she sat me down.

"Sorry but something odd just came up," she said showing me her computer screen.

The screen showed a picture of a sheep, and the room the sheep was in looked a lot like the back room of the lab where she had kept me when I had… transformed. I looked like a sheep, an odd sheep, but still a sheep. Perhaps I was still changing at that point.

"I hope this doesn't traumatize you too much," said Calamity.

"What is so important?" I asked, "Did this get out onto the internet or something."

"No," said Calamity. "This is being kept private. But there is something else on the internet."

She showed a different image, of a rather similar-looking sheep in a pen. It looked a bit like the one of me a moment ago, and also rang a few bells to an article I saw on Twitface.

"Hold on," I said, "Is that one of the breeds of smart sheep from the nearby farm, the Sapi sheep?"

"Yeah," said Calamity. "It does look familiar, doesn't it… I will put them side by side so you can judge better."

The two sheep did look very similar. I began to mentally run through various scenarios; she could not be suggesting what I thought she was.

"Please tell me you aren't suggesting that these sheep are transformed, people," I said.

"Well… I know it sounds crazy to say it out loud but it might be the case," said Calamity. "After all the Sapi sheep can respond to fairly complicated instructions, on par with what we might expect of a very young child, in multiple languages. Mostly in English, but some have responded to Spanish commands. This in spite of the fact that no one on the farm the breed originated on spoke Spanish.

"Add to the fact that there are no records of the breeding up to this point, the general secrecy of the farm's staff, that no one else in the world got sheep anywhere close to this intelligent, it's not enough to make accusations, but… well it does turn some wheels."

"Turn some wheels?" I asked.

"Raise some eyebrows," said Calamity, awkwardly looking away from me. "I don't know why I said anything about turning wheels."

I blinked a few times.

"Anyway," said Calamity. "What do you think of all this? I know you made the same connection I did but…"

"It would be… are you sure about this… how would we even go about proving this?"

"No idea."

"Well, that's a good start then."

Calamity stood up and walked around her office. "I would recommend scoping out the farm. We could maybe get an idea of what is actually going on from that."

"I don't care what you offer me," I said. "I am not going to walk around a creepy farm, in the middle of the night. Besides I would probably get in trouble for trespassing."

"But would you do it in broad daylight, having bought a ticket?" asked Calamity.

I paused for a moment, "Would we even find anything?"

"Maybe enough that we could eventually go to the actual police with something. If we find anything." Calamity sat back down. "If they are keeping an eye out for people who might know a thing or two you would be less out of place. If you go on Saturday it would probably be at its most busy, you would get lost in the crowd."

"Hold on Calamity, I haven't agreed to anything, why should I go."

"I will pay overtime for eight hours if you do."

"Ok, that works."

So Saturday came and went and I didn't go because it was raining. We changed plans to the Saturday after, but then Sue called and we had to spend an afternoon with her. We did mention our plans, and she helpfully informed us that going through their garbage was surprisingly legal. After that Saturday it was raining again, and my parents came by from Colorado to visit the Saturday after that. Then finally just one week before classes started again, I got a chance to go to the farm.

On that Saturday I started out. Dr. Calamity told me to save all receipts and she would reimburse me for "reasonable expenses". Such as getting into the farm, gas, and such. My first stop was at the local Brew HAHA to get some coffee.

After ordering one "As dark and bitter as my soul" and then paying for and receiving a white chocolate mocha with extra cream and sugar, I got started on my drive listening to an audiobook. My destination was *Leaf It To Me* Farm and Museum. It was where the smart sheep lived and were bred, and according to Sue, recipient of multiple lawsuits revolving around genetic copyright, only a few of which were from Windbreakers who liked to sue people who couldn't fight back when their GMO pollen got into someone else's soybeans.

The drive was two and a half hours each way, and passed three towns, two of which you could miss if you blinked at the wrong moment. Then I finally arrived at *Leaf It To Me*, paid the twelve ninety-nine entrance fee, and got busy looking around. Sue and Calamity wanted me to take a look around and take pictures. Calamity, because "we might find something interesting in an unexpected place" and Sue, because "I smell blood in the water."

The museum itself was not air-conditioned, but it was still moderately comfortable at the end of summer. Walking around, I started in the "Glow house" a greenhouse where all the leaves of all the plants glowed. Just like the trees they had been growing in the Netherlands and now elsewhere in Europe, and soon in parts of the U.S. Still the sign on the wall claimed "Despite claims to the contrary by Dutch scientists, *Leaf It To Me* developed and grew these plants on our own."

The "Glow house" was not particularly special to someone who had been following genetics for half a decade. But it was still interesting in a way. I went onwards to the spider goats. Goats that in this case had 8 legs, and produced spider silk instead of milk. Again the information panels claimed this was an invention by *Leaf It To Me*. In reality this innovation was created nearby in Utah, not in Montana.

From there I visited the Beef-Steak tomato garden. Literal Beef-steak. This was an Indian creation, that is to say, from India, not from a Native American. Anyway, the idea was to create a source of beef that would be… vegan… vegetarian? The same lab eventually did something with chicken and fish. Some Hindus and Buddhists shrugged and said that this was fine. Some did not; vegetarians and vegans were equally split. Though both sides would agree that this development came from a prestigious lab in India, and not in some hick's garage in the middle of nowhere. That is everyone except *Leaf It To Me,* who not only refuted the claim that this was developed in India but was also quite racist about it. Below the many racist comments that I do not feel comfortable repeating, and barely felt comfortable reading, was a paper note saying "It's just a joke, stop complaining snowflakes."

I ignored that, and also a person complaining about the treatment of the meat-producing plants being unethical. Seriously she was holding up a sign saying "All Meat has Felling." Yes, she misspelled feelings, and also told anyone who so much as looked at the meat fruits that "You're a Murderer". She also questioned a small child, "Did you know your parents are horrible people?" when one of her parents mentioned that this might be acceptable for a vegan friend.

Anyway, I was onto the main attraction, the Sapi Sheep. I swear the first thing I heard was one bleating out an SOS in Morris code. I don't know much but I know three fast, three slow, and three fast = SOS. Still, the conditions looked like any petting zoo. Wooden fence, pathways everywhere, food dispenser. The only major difference was there was an area where people were taking turns asking the sheep math questions.

"The Sheep is wrong I tell you," said a patron, a woman whose looks seemed to match her personality.

"Not according to the calculator," said a worker who looked tired, beaten up, and like all that she wanted to do was go home.

"Then your calculator is also wrong!"

"It's not."

"I know my numbers. Five Times Five Is Thirty-Five," said the woman shouting for no apparent reason.

"No." said another patron, a man who looked even worse than the woman. "Five times five is thirty, not thirty-five. Get it right, you moron."

"No, five times five is fifteen," said someone else.

I looked toward one of the sheep "You're smarter than most of the people here aren't you?"

The sheep nodded, I think I saw a tear in its eye.

I looked over at the argument.

"Ma'am you need to calm down," said what looked like a very tired security guard.

"WHY DON'T YOU GIVE ME MY MONEY BACK?!" said the woman from earlier. "I WAS PROMISED SMART SHEEP, AND THESE SHEEP ARE STUPID."

"Ma'am," said the guard, who looked male, mid-twenties, wearing a black uniform. "We don't offer refunds except in the case of bad weather or injury."

The woman looked him in the eye, grabbed the fence, and tried to pull it apart. It didn't work. So she rammed her head into the fence. The guard tried to pull her off and called for backup but she fought him, seemingly, for the right to bash her head in on the fence.

Seeing that, I decided that I could do a more sensible thing, and talk to this sheep.

"You understand English?" I asked.

The sheep baaaed and nodded.

"I guess it would be baaad if you didn't," I said.

The sheep looked at me like I had just told the worst pun ever. Honestly, it may have had a point. I sat down as close as I could get to the sheep through the fence.

"Are you from around here?"

The sheep shook its head.

"What about… Somewhere in North America?"

The sheep paused for a second, and nodded.

"Were you born in the U.S.?"

The sheep nodded.

"But not on this farm?"

Sheep nods.

"Did the people here teach you English?"

Sheep, head shake.

"Did you know when you came here?"

Nod.

I looked around nervously to see if anyone was watching me.

"I'm injured," said the woman from earlier, now with a small cut on her forehead that was bleeding rather nastily, "I demand a refund." And two security guards wrestled her out of the area.

Elsewhere a massive argument to the nature of five times five had broken out with two more security guards trying to keep everyone calm; the crowd apparently indifferent to the chaos behind them. Seeing all this, I figured that me sitting on the ground and talking to a sheep would go unnoticed.

"So… did you learn English… on your own?"

The sheep looked at me for a second then nodded.

"… this will sound crazy…" I looked around to make sure no one was looking at me in particular, "Were you always a sheep?"

Head shake.

"Where you once human?"

Nodding, enthusiastic nodding.

"Ok… just to prove you are definitely understanding me, can you go find… a stick or something in your pen, ohhh, or a bit of straw or hay from your pen?"

The sheep nodded, ran off, and returned with a mouth full of hay.

"Thanks," I said to the sheep, "Do you want help?"

The sheep nodded.

"I can't promise anything, but I will see what I can do."

The sheep baa-ed in response, I think I saw a few more tears.

I finally got up and wandered around a bit more. There was one more exhibit, they were trying to claim the duck-billed platypus as something genetically modified, and then I had to exit through the gift shop. Honestly, I had a quick look around and nothing caught my eye as worth it even if they were sold for zero dollars and zero cents.

I then got to Hank and drove away to a nearby restaurant for lunch. Had a salad which I previously didn't do, but have liked more since my own transformation. Then I made a trip to a battleground, a place where government forces squared off with native Americans. It was much more educational, and it didn't feel good. A little reminder of the tragedies and atrocities my country is built on.

Then it was dinner, and one last thing for Calamity and Sue, checking *Leaf It To Me*'s garbage. Though I had to wait a little while before it would be dark, so off to a random forest to kill a few hours. Then finally back to *Leaf It To Me*; it was dark though still twilight. I had a flashlight and walked from where I parked to *Leaf It To Me*. Once there I found their dumpster, I wasn't going to dig too much, but I had thick latex gloves with me, and with them on I could poke around for a bit. A few cars drove by, and I ducked out of the way for each of them just in case, but nothing seemed to be troublesome. I didn't see anything odd, but I photographed everything with my phone and grabbed a few things that stood out. After bagging a few things, a broken beaker, a few syringes, a few t-shirts that had seen better days, and some Petri dishes, I heard a car drive up.

I ducked behind a nearby bush as this car, rather than go past, approached the museum/farm. It looked like a van, an old beat-up van. Two people got out of it; I was just barely close enough to hear them.

"Where are they?" asked the driver.

"Jay said he would be here soon," said the guy riding shotgun, and seemingly carrying an actual shotgun.

"He was supposed to be here by now, how is he late again?"

"He got stopped by police again. They insisted on talking to him, he had to get the lawyer to help him out."

"Rob, do we really need that piece of garbage?"

"Considering that what we are doing is actually illegal? Like very illegal, yes, we need that piece of garbage. Also, don't say piece of garbage to the lawyer's face alright."

"Why not, considering he is a piece of garbage?"

"Because he is the piece of garbage that is keeping us out of prison. Seriously if people knew the truth about the sheep, then Windbreakers will be the least of our concerns. We need that piece of garbage."

"Doesn't mean he is not a piece of…"

A second car showed up, two people got out. The driver was carrying a lot of rope, in the dark, I couldn't make much out, though he looked familiar; the only passenger was carrying a briefcase.

"Please tell me the serums are actually ready this time," said the first driver, Rob, "We can't have another situation where we have these people we've stolen in the basement for a week again."

"It's ready," said the guy with a briefcase.

By this time, I had my phone recording video, I was just barely peeking out of the corner of the bush. Just enough to get a clear view.

The guy carrying rope looked behind him. "Let's get this over with," he said, in a voice that was all too familiar. When they said Jay, did they mean Jay Walker? The guy whose mistake made me a sheep. I took a moment to calm myself.

The first driver then opened up the side door of the van, shotgun-guy was there, pointing the gun at the general direction of the inside. I heard the sounds of muffled screaming, human screams.

"Quiet," said shotgun man, "If you want to live you will do exactly as we say. Stay still, Jay will be getting you."

Jay, yes that Jay, I saw his face, before he got inside the van, I snuck out a bit to see him tying the rope around a woman's hands, and a minute later that woman, partly tied up and gagged, was dragged out of the van. Rob then closed the van door, and Jay, shotgun man, and briefcase man followed the group in. They did the same thing with the other seven passengers, four more women, and three men. Each one gagged and partly tied up. Once done, Jay got back into the van. Shotgun and Briefcase were just standing around. The van started up and after a moment was moving in my general direction.

I stopped recording and focused on hiding. There was nowhere to go but behind a single bush, a holly, nothing else to quickly dive behind. The van drove past me into a parking spot behind the dumpster. Then Jay got back out and started walking in my general direction. I didn't know if he saw me, but I was way too exposed. I could move to the other side of the bush, but that's where his three friends were waiting. Jay is getting closer, I needed to do something so I dove under the bush.

Jay looked right at me, did he see me, was it too late, was I too loud? It was the same Jay Walker who leered at me and got me transformed into a sheep. If he thought I got him fired, would he make good on his threats? Am I about to become their next victim? I was paying attention to every noise I was making, I was just wondering if my breathing was too loud and giving me away, when....

"Damn raccoons," said Jay, then he started walking again, past the bush and past me. Then he met up with his three buddies.

"Take us home," said Rob, and he and his three buddies got into the car with Jay driving. They then drove off.

Once they were gone, I took a deep breath, then realized just how prickly and thorny the bush was. I carefully worked my way out.

"Ow, ow... ow.... ow," I said as every single thorn in this bush had its way with me.

I then brushed myself off and walked back to my car. I was alone, I thought I was safe enough here in the middle of nowhere, but now I was freaking out. Someone might find me and hurt me, I walked quickly to the car. If a police officer found me... would they accept my explanation..., did I have an explanation?

I got to Hank, and took a deep breath, safe at last. I started him up and began the long drive home.

CHAPTER 4

I got home and tried to breathe, then I uploaded all my phone's data onto my computer. I took a moment to worry about tomorrow, being up so late, then remembered that tomorrow was Sunday, and that I had the day off. Then I realized that technically it was Sunday now as it was after midnight. After getting my data onto my computer I emailed everything to Sue and Calamity. Finally, I let myself have the freak out that had been building up since the van.

When that was done I tried to go to bed, but my heart was still racing, so I got up, and got on my computer for a while to try and calm myself, I checked Twitface several times but most of my friends were asleep. I looked for videos, I played some games, and I found myself looking for apartments near me with security systems. Then I finally grew tired enough to try and sleep.

Sunday was uneventful and I rested. I actually didn't wake up until noon. I saw that Sue, and Calamity had the files, and Sue said something about forwarding the video to the authorities. She also said that Jay's father had assaulted some poor retail worker and was in jail, for a while at least. And also that with the email he sent me he was probably staying there a while.

On Monday I was working with some data when I heard a knock on the lab door.

"I got it," said Calamity, getting out of her office to answer the door.

"Hello, I am Richard from the Bureau Of Odd Biology," said our unexpected guest wearing a suit and tie.

"Oh… Dick from B.O.O.B," said Calamity. somehow managing that with a straight face, I hid mine to stifle a laugh. "Are you done chasing Bigfoot?"

Richard sighed, "Ma'am this is important."

"So was, apparently, a report on Bigfoot. So important in fact was it that when I tried to help you by giving you all my camera trap photos, and Bigfoot failed to appear, you arrested me for not helping you hard enough."

"Well maybe if you idiots would actually look you could find him but that is not what I am here about today."

"Is it the Loch-ness monster?"

"If I had half a mind to, I would arrest you for that."

"I am already in contact with a lawyer, good luck getting that to stick."

"OHHH, you have a lawyer, well la de da, it doesn't matter, I wanted to ask about the incident."

"What incident?"

"The incident where one of your lab assistants got turned into a sheep, probably an idiot who didn't read a safety label."

"I take it you did not actually read the incident report."

"Why should I?"

"Because you would know two things, one, the incident occurred due to a spill that another then-assistant spilled in the food safe fridge…"

"What the hell does food-safe mean?"

"You would know three things, what I just went over, what food-safe meant, and what the lab assistant actually looked like. You might have avoided calling her an idiot."

"Hello," I said, "I am the former sheep."

"But… she's human?" said Richard.

"If you had read the incident report you would have known four things," said Calamity.

"I don't need to read incident reports. You sound like my boss. I just want to talk with you… and your assistant, in my office."

"Why?"

"Because this whole accident reminds me of a top-secret government experiment. It's too similar. I need to know how you got the data. Did you steal it?"

"One, I didn't steal any information, and two, this conversation is over until my lawyer gives her approval."

"How do I know your lawyer?"

"It's entirely possible I mentioned her in the incident report."

Calamity then closed the door.

Then she stood by the door. "Give it three seconds," she said.

Then there was more knocking.

Calamity opened the door, Richard was still there. "Just come down to my office, we can talk."

"Do you have an arrest warrant?" asked Calamity.

"I don't. Why would I need one? This is just a chat," said Richard.

"You nearly got me in jail after just-a-chat last time, and all because I failed to provide what I didn't actually have. Contact my lawyer if you want to talk."

She closed the door again but Richard bashed into it to get inside.

"Ma'am this really is important," he said.

"Then go back to your B.O.O.B. office and read the incident report, who knows maybe the answer you need is there. If not, then call my lawyer and we can arrange a time."

"Now is good."

"Do you have a warrant?"

"Why would I need one?"

"Because if you don't, I will have to ask you to leave."

"No, I am not leaving."

Calamity got out her phone.

"What are you doing you stupid woman?" asked Richard.

"You will see," said Calamity.

Then she talked into the phone, "Hello… Yeah you know Dick from B.O.O.B.… You got it… Five minutes… Thank you." She then hung up.

A few minutes later Richards's phone went off.

"Hello, Richard Head here." He went from slouched to in full attention. "You what, but… OK… I will come back."

He hung up, "Have a good day." Then he left.

Calamity closed the door and came to me.

"He nearly got me into trouble the first time we met."

"You knew each other?" I asked.

"He was convinced that I knew something about a cryptid, yes it was Bigfoot. I thought he was just an idiot, but he was part of an actual government organization. Nearly got in trouble but John got me in touch with Sue, who helped get him off my back. Turns out his gut told him I had a photograph of a Bigfoot.

I raised an eyebrow, "So he tried to arrest you for not having a photograph that didn't exist?"

Calamity nodded, "He will probably be back, don't talk to him without Sue by your side, I made the mistake of trying to cooperate with him, but he seems to translate 'I don't know' or 'I can't help you there', or even 'that's impossible for me to do', to 'I have everything you need but will not give it to you for my own selfish reasons'."

"How did he nearly get you in trouble?"

"He was convinced that a camera trap I set out had caught a picture of a Bigfoot. This was back when I was in undergrad, and he was insistent that I give him the whole reel. I thought that if I cooperated he would see that the camera trap had nothing but deer and raccoons and go away. So I sent him a copy of the photos the camera took. When Bigfoot failed to show up he decided that I had taken the one picture he needed out, and arrested me. I called John, John called Sue, Sue stopped me from trying to talk my way out and got me home that night. Two years later a judge verbally chewed Dick out before telling him to leave me alone, but he did that in legalese."

"How did he get into a government bureau?"

Calamity shrugged, "Honestly I think that B.O.O.B. is where they send the screw-ups that they can't just fire."

"That would explain the name," I said.

Calamity nodded.

Sue kept in touch, as Richard tried to get an arrest warrant on us, and failed. He then emailed me asking me to come by for a talk. I did as Calamity instructed and referred him to Sue to set that up. He argued and moaned for a week. Then he tried to have us arrested again, failed, and then finally got in touch with Sue to set up a meeting. While that was happening we spent a lot of time talking to Sue. She said she was preparing something.

Sue, Calamity, and I eventually got together with Richard.

"You didn't need to bring a lawyer with you," said Richard. "I am not accusing you of anything."

"Well, then there should be no problem with me sitting in," said Sue. "After all if this is just a chat then surely there would be nothing to hide from the lawyer, right?"

Richard smiled, looked at me, and said "It's common knowledge, you know, that the Venn-diagram of lawyers and a**holes is a circle right?"

"I have represented many a**holes who could sue you for unfairly comparing them to lawyers," said Sue.

"They are also idiots," said Richard still looking at me.

"Do you want to increase my business?" asked Sue, looking directly at Richard.

Richard sighed. "How did you get that video?" he said to me.

"She visited the exterior of the property after dark. She did not trespass; everything she did was on or concerning public property and therefore legal," said Sue.

"I wasn't asking you, you B****," said Richard.

"She said everything as clearly as I could have," I said.

"Yes but I am not interviewing her, I am interviewing you," said Richard. "Answer the question."

"I was doing exactly what Sue just said I was," I said.

"Why were you on the property?"

"She was looking for evidence of general genetic misconduct as a citizen," said Sue. "She only visited the interior during the hours it was open to the public."

Richard sighed.

"And you," he said, turning to Calamity. "Where did you get the serum that turned people into sheep?"

"She developed it," said Sue.

"Really," said Richard looking at Sue. "No outside help? No notes from someone else?"

"She is keeping track of the supplies she used and the work she has cited. All are publicly available and what she purchased she is licensed to purchase, or again is publicly available. She has sent me a full copy of all the supplies and previous data used. If you ask nicely, I can send you a copy as well."

Richard sighed and looked to Sue, "No shady black-market deals, nothing off the record that you could quietly grab... do you really expect me to believe that?"

"My clients are working in a field that requires total transparency," said Sue. "If others are to be able to copy and make use of their work then they have to understand what their work actually is. Thus every step of the way must be recorded so that others can build on it. If they used any supply that they did not disclose then all they have done would be for nothing."

"There are always secrets."

"Not always; maybe with your line of work, but not with my clients."

Richard looked at me, "I would like to ask Ms. Night some personal questions."

"Only if you understand that she is under no obligation to answer them," said Sue. "And that I can and will end this interview if she indicates to me, or appears to me to be uncomfortable with your questions."

Richard sighed, "Ms. Night did you know..." He smiled, "Did your parents ever tell you that you were not... hold on, I got my words messed up... Did your parents ever tell you that they were not actually your REAL parents?"

"They are my real parents," I said. "The fact that they adopted me is secondary to that."

Richards's smile suddenly faded, "Well… that must have been a shock… surely this took some time for you to… recollect and learn to trust them after that reveal."

"I think I knew I was adopted since as far back as I can remember," I said. "I don't think there was ever a time in which they did not state that I was adopted but loved all the same."

"Well… have you ever been curious about your real parents?"

"They are my real parents, again, the fact that they adopted me doesn't make them any less real."

"Be careful how you word your questions," said Sue to Richard.

"Alright, what about biological parents," said Richard to me. "Did they ever tell you the truth about them?"

"They told me they didn't know who my bio parents were," I said. "The agency they got me from said that I was given up anonymously."

"Surely you would have wanted to meet them," said Richard, sweating.

"Not in particular," I said.

"Re-really?"

"Nope."

"But… ahhh I get it you must think they are jerks?"

"She makes no assumptions," interjected Sue. "That she cares not to meet her biological parents just means that she has considered and rejected the thought of tracking them down. This could be for any number of reasons, some of which might be subconscious. Maybe she is worried that they would be jerks, or maybe she is assuming that they could not care for a child such as herself at the time. Maybe the mother was part of a conservative family and had a baby out of wedlock in secret. Or maybe she has decided that if her biological parents wanted to be a part of her life, they would have and that her adoptive parents are good enough."

"What if I could tell her right now," said Richard, "What if I know?"

"That would be up to her," said Sue. "And it only matters if you actually know."

"I do know," said Richard, "I was there."

Sue looked to me, I got that she wanted me to say the next word.

"Go on," I said.

"To start, it's a long story, do you know what demographic collapse is?" said Richard.

I looked to Sue who gave me a nod, Calamity looked smug; she taught me this topic.

"It is the result of birth rate decline due to a number of factors in developed countries," I began. "Mainly as families get the resources to control family size, and as outside circumstances encourage smaller family size, most of these factors being the things that make developed countries a nice place to live."

"Ahh, so you do have a brain in there," said Richard.

"One more comment like that and this interview will be over," said Sue.

Richard turned to her and glared, "You can't just…"

"Oh I can, you have nothing to arrest her on, therefore if she is being made uncomfortable she can just leave, and another comment like that and as her legal counsel, I will terminate this interview. Are we clear?" said Sue.

Richard continued to glare at her, then he sighed, "Yes." He then turned to me, "Anyway we were trying to combat it by using a medical treatment that would transform a variety of animals into humans. These new humans could then take on the jobs and roles in society that natural humans didn't want to do anymore."

"If you were really transforming animals into people then wouldn't they still require training and practice in order to walk, speak, and to act human, much less perform human jobs?" I asked.

Richard's face changed to a grim smile, "I got you, how could you have known that unless you were there?!"

"She simply spotted a flaw in your plan," said Sue.

"It took us years to work out that, do you expect that she could do that in five seconds?" asked Richard.

Sue paused, looked at him, and said "One, what made you think these transformed humans would have those skills? Two, if you try that in front of a jury they will laugh and declare my client not guilty. And three, the only people who couldn't spot that flaw right away would be the kind who have only two brain cells… both fighting for third place.

Richard fumed for a moment, then calmed down "I don't know how you figured it out," said Richard. "But I will find out… regardless you apparently know what ruined the project."

I looked to Sue. She nodded.

"So you did run into the obvious problem?" she said.

Richard sighed heavily and glared even harder; I thought he was going to explode. "Regardless, we changed tactics, we tried to instead transform newborns, these children could then learn as they grew up."

I decided to not ask how they found people to raise these kids, given how he reacted previously to my question.

"Nothing smart to say," said Richard, "You don't want to show off again. Well we had trouble raising these kids, and the project was abandoned. But we kept track of where they went. One, that used to be a foal, was adopted by the Night family, and was named Trixie... sound familiar?"

I kept silent.

Sue got up and tapped me on the shoulder.

"If you knew anything about this, now would be a good time to let me know," she whispered into my ear.

"No, I have seen my adoption papers, they didn't say anything other than I was anonymously given up," I whispered back.

"Ok, good, don't say anything," said Sue.

"So you do know?" said Richard. "They must have told you."

I kept quiet.

"Actually Ms. Night has informed me that her adoption paperwork said she was given up anonymously," said Sue. "So she had no idea any of this was the case. Can we see the paperwork on your end?"

Richard glared at Sue. "That's classified," he said.

"Then, without proof, I will have no choice but to conclude that you are lying... therefore I will have to terminate this interview, and formally request that you do not harass either of my clients anymore. I will be submitting a request to a judge by the end of the day, I expect that you shall have a Cease and Desist on your desk within the week."

"You can't just go, she knew about the project, I am sure, I can feel it in my gut."

"I can feel it in my gut only works in cop shows. What you have is nothing more than a guess, grasped at a straw so loose that it was already in the water when you started looking for something to pull you up."

"She knew what shut the project down."

"And I can convince any jury in the world that what she said was an educated guess. They might even make the guess themselves, with this in hand she gets declared not guilty and I get to drain your department's time energy, and money to make you look bad to your superiors. Cause you made a claim that got laughed out of court."

She turned to us, "Calamity, Night, let's get out of here."

I stood up, as did Calamity. Richard began to sweat harder.

"Wait," he said. "I gave you classified information; I can't let you go unless you sign a non-disclosure agreement."

"You can't make us stay," said Sue. "Non-disclosure agreements are meant to be given before you find out anything. If we fail to sign you tell us nothing; if given now it is given under duress and is illegitimate. If you refuse to let us go then you will have to charge us with something. I doubt that you could make knowledge of classified information stick when you told it to us without checking or getting us clearance first. Though I am sure your boss could fire you for this."

Richard gulped.

"We will be leaving, expect my Cease and Detest to arrive by the end of the week."

We left the building with no issues and Sue drove us to her office.

"If he calls or emails you again let me know, don't speak to him without me except to say that you won't say anything until you have legal counsel," said Sue. "I will be getting that cease and desist if I can, if nothing else these details should get him in trouble with his boss. Any questions?"

"Do you really think you can get a Cease and Desist?" asked Calamity.

"Maybe," said Sue. "If nothing else his poor work should be enough for him to find himself on the wrong end of a lecture from someone, maybe a judge, maybe his boss, probably both. If nothing else he told us that he gave us classified information before vetting us, not a good look."

"Do you believe what he said?" I asked, "The whole 'you were born a horse' story?"

"Given what we have seen, maybe, but just because it might be true doesn't mean it is. He could be telling a lie; I don't know why he would, but he could be."

"So...?"

"I wouldn't bet money either way. If you find something about that let me know before you do anything else."

"We might be able to test that," said Calamity. "I... as an apology for having to deal with some... issues... received the very best of the next-gen DNA sequencing lab kit. We need to test it out any way... we might be able to find something."

"How much would that cost?" I asked.

"There was a mix-up, and they ordered more supplies than I would normally use in a year. We have more set to come in at the end of the year so I can afford to burn a little," said Calamity.

"Convenient isn't it?" said Sue.

"Yeah... how much are you costing Calamity?" I asked.

"None," said Sue.

"The university pays for all legal expenses as a bonus," said Calamity. "That fund is actually what is paying for Sue to prosecute the board for Mr. Walker."

"Nice," I said.

"Indeed," said Sue.

CHAPTER 5

A few days later I was looking at the results for the test Calamity did.

"I know that might be a bit shocking," she said. "But I double-checked… it's there."

"A sequence of DNA unique to *Equus caballus*, but in my genome," I said, staring at the results.

"Yes," said Calamity. "Guess Richard wasn't lying about everything after all."

We sat in silence for a while.

"But… what about sheep DNA, did you find any of that?" I asked.

"Yes," said Calamity. "But like the horse DNA, it's a very small amount. I could say that ninety-nine-point-nine percent of your DNA is human, but that implies that you have less human DNA than you actually do. If I didn't know to look for it, I doubt I would have seen it."

"What about you… could this be normal?" I asked, "If it's so little that you wouldn't notice if you went looking, maybe it's in everyone."

"Based on some public DNA sequences… no, you are… unique in that regard."

I slumped in the chair, this felt very odd, I wouldn't call it devastating, but it was disturbing.

"Listen," said Calamity. "It doesn't change anything about who you are. You are the same Trixie Night that I knew yesterday, the same person you always were. It doesn't change who you are. This might be an interesting tidbit, but as far as anyone on the street would be concerned, you are fully human. No less real than anyone else."

"Ok… that makes me feel a bit better," I said, "I should probably get started on whatever we need done today."

"If you need time take it," said Calamity.

"Actually, I think some work might be good for me, not difficult or complex, something that requires just enough effort to feel really satisfying when it's done," I said.

Calamity nodded, "Well I have done some more sequencing on transformed rats. You could check the proto-oncogenes to see if they are undamaged. But if that is too close to home…"

"I think I can handle it," I said. I also wanted to see just how much DNA was left behind but I didn't say that.

"Ok," said Calamity. She got me some files and I got to work.

I scanned through them, quickly checking for frog DNA. It was there, it wasn't much but it was there. In the end, I collected the data she wanted on the proto-oncogenes and quickly ran it through a statistics program she set up for me, and… compared it to the control. No change… This was also good news for me as damaged proto-oncogenes can lead to cancer. So, knowing that my risks were probably normal was nice.

I went home feeling satisfied, just what I needed to get my mind off things, a project done. I had dinner and played a computer game or two.

The rest of the week was quiet which was good as it allowed me to look up at the ceiling while trying to sleep, and contemplate that I was once a horse. If that was a bad thing in general, or for me, after all, what life would I have had as a horse? I would probably be in old age by now, no understanding of my life, probably just being trained and ridden as a beast of burden. But I might have also been happy, and blissfully unaware of my short lifespan, so no existential dread. Also, no classes or jobs to worry about, no rent, no taxes, so maybe not so bad. I struggled to decide whether I had been given a great gift, or cheated.

The beginning of next week, Monday, we had another court date. Richard got a judge, Lou Phol, to speak to him.

Richard spoke first. "These individuals have knowledge of classified information."

"Only because he told us," said Sue.

"… Well… She," said Richard pointing to me. "Knew classified information I did not tell her."

"She determined a very obvious flaw in a past plan," said Sue. "One almost anyone could have determined based on what he told us."

"Tell me," said Judge Phol to Richard. "What did she know?"

"That's classified," said Richard.

"So I can't judge if what Ms. Sue is saying is true or not, because you won't tell me the exact flaw?"

Richard looked stunned.

"Therefore, unless you can provide reasonable evidence that she found this secret illegally, then I will have to assume she is innocent."

Richard fumbled.

"And according to the defense, you told them the rest of the classified information, without getting them cleared first," said Phol. "If that is the case, this is your failure, not her failure."

Richard stammered, "I…I…Give me something."

"No," said Phol, "I am throwing this case out of court. Mr. Richard Head, if you want to get a case like this through, you better have evidence next time of the wrongdoing of your opponent. No charges."

Richard fumed.

"Adjourned," said Phol, smashing the gavel down.

With that dealt with, it was on to thing two, in another part of the courthouse.

Sue led us through the hallways to an office and knocked.

"Come in," said a voice from inside.

"No way," said Sue at a whisper.

She opened the door and inside sat a man who looked somewhat surprised.

"Errum. Have a seat," he said.

A moment later it was time for introductions.

"Dr. Calamity, Ms. Night, this is officer Sick Em."

"Yes, our last name is the same, I am her husband," said Officer Sick.

"Will that be a problem?" asked Calamity.

"We have worked together before," said Sue. "As long as you two aren't suspects this should be OK."

"They aren't," said Officer Sick. "I am mostly worried about them being witnesses. I think you can represent their interests without conflicting with me."

There was an awkward silence.

"Anyway," said Sick. "I got the video you sent in, and I am concerned. We should have enough for a warrant."

"What is the issue then?" asked Calamity.

"The sheep thing is the issue," said Sick. "The video is ample evidence that a human trafficking operation is occurring. I expect to have a warrant by tomorrow, and the raid is being planned to occur on Wednesday. But if what you say is true, then many of our victims are now sheep."

Sick stood up and paced behind his desk. "I find this hard to believe, and so would any judge. But if it is true, *Leaf It To Me* has been selling these Sapi Sheep. If they are, or were, people then they are victims who need rescue. We could track down the sale's receipts and, if what your reports suggest is possible, return them to human. So I don't want to discount the possibility, especially as, I have been told, that while this is new research, it has been discussed in the scientific community. I received a report from who I now know to be my wife on the matter, so I have reason to believe that this transformation thing is not entirely implausible. We also know… suspect… that *Leaf It To Me* has been known to… borrow scientific innovations without permission, and the idea that this might just be another illegal activity is possible. Though thus far… they have had worryingly good lawyers."

Sick looked at Sue.

"I will consider helping… if I can," she said.

Sick nodded, "You have a duty to them first I know… anyway it will require some substantial evidence that this is possible. Then we might be able to track down and rescue the Sapi sheep sold by *Leaf It To Me* if that is what is happening. But I do not have the ability to investigate this with my own labs… but you do. I can shut down the human trafficking without you, but if you truly believe that people are being turned into sheep… as hard as that is to say… then I will need you to show that to me, and to help me fight to rescue them."

"I'm in," said Calamity. "If that is what is happening, I can prove it."

"What about you," said Sick, looking to me.

"I will think about it," I said.

Sick nodded, "Ok. If nothing else, I may need you to come in as an in-person witness when this goes to court."

I nodded, "I know."

"Good," said Sick. "Well I think that is it. Any questions?"

There were none.

"Ok, I just need a way to contact you… and then we can head out… it is lunchtime, my treat."

Thursday evening, I heard about a raid on *Leaf It To Me*, though the news seemed confused. Friday morning, I was meeting with Calamity to discuss how things would change with classes next week, but early into our meeting, there was a knock on the door. It was Sick.

"Hello," he said, "I have told my wife I needed to speak to you; as per our agreements she is on her way."

Then Sue's car pulled into a parking lot. "I am here," she said, "What is going on?"

"I need their help… and I need you to sign off on me asking this of them."

"Ok. What do you need help with?"

Sick turned to Calamity, "May I come in to discuss this with you inside please?"

"Umm," said Calamity who looked to Sue, who nodded, "Sure."

We sat down and Sick looked to Calamity with eyes I could only describe as pleading, watering.

"Can you make a formula to turn a Sapi sheep back into a human?" he asked. "Do you have that now?"

"I can get some for you by the end of tomorrow. But I don't have any now."

"What would you need to get it done by today?" asked Sick. "Seriously sooner is better… please!"

"Doesn't work that way, can't rush it, it's like cooking a turkey, if the instructions say three-fifty for four hours you can't make it done with six-hundred for two hours."

"Damn, I hope I can at least convince you to work weekends…"

"I will have some ready by the end of the day tomorrow," said Calamity.

Sick looked like he was about to cry, I could see tears starting to form.

"Ok, I will tell you where to deliver it… please get started… make as much as you can. Bring me a list of costs so I can reimburse you." He then left.

"Sorry," said Sue who followed her husband. "Are you OK?" were the only words I heard from her.

Calamity looked at me and shrugged, and we finished our meeting and got to work. Luckily the formula required little supervision at each step, so we could make a lot even on a busy day.

"Sorry I will have to ask you to come in tomorrow… but if you do, I will give you Monday and Tuesday off," said Calamity.

"Deal," I said, knowing that classes started Wednesday, and my hours would be much shorter now that classes were beginning.

The work was dull and repetitive, but we did make a mountain of the stuff.

We arrived to the delivery point, the local precinct, and Sue lead us inside.

"OUT OF THE WAY," shouted Sick from across the room. "MAKE A HOLE"

"You got it?" he asked Calamity.

"The first vial," said Calamity. "I have twenty more, each is good for one treatment."

"How do we do that?" asked Sick.

"One vial, ingested orally, each vial is about one milliliter."

Sick nodded, "Twenty… can I ask you to take some time to teach the forensic team how to make this later, also where is that receipt for your reimbursement?"

Calamity handed Sick a piece of paper. Sick took one look at it and then handed it to an officer nearby. "Write a check for the money she spent."

"Yes sir." The officer nodded before walking away.

Sick turned to Calamity, "I also need to ask you to examine a sample. I want you to compare it to what you made."

"I may have just given my best lab assistant Monday and Tuesday off, and I can't ask her to come in tomorrow," said Calamity.

"I thought that Trixie was your only lab assistant," said Sick.

"She is that too… though we started the summer with two… I fired the other one so hard I think his great-grandkids felt it," said Calamity with a smile.

"About that," said Sue. "I need your two statements on any… sexually inappropriate statements Mr. Jay Walker may have said… or anything he did along those lines. Turns out he might have gotten a pass on… 'having non-consensual sex' because he 'was just a kid' and he might have also done it again. This is particularly important because while Trixie got footage of him at *Leaf It To Me*, my husband was not able to locate him so far."

"Right," I said thinking about how he leered at me so often.

"He was not at his home," said Sick. "And his known friends and family had no information on his whereabouts."

Sue nodded, "Also, I need to talk to Calamity in particular about his father... turns out he also left a trail of blood that is now attracting other lawyers. I want to get a bite in while I have the chance," said Sue.

"Anyway," said Sick. "While my wife takes on her true form as a shark I would like to ask if I can get on your schedule Dr. Calamity? It will probably take me some time on my end but if you could get me something in a week or two?"

"I think we can manage that," said Calamity. "And about the serum class?"

"I will let you know when the forensic team has time to learn... or if they can... but we will need more of the transformation drink... lots more."

"How much?"

"That's the bad thing, I don't know yet." Sick turned to me, "One last thing... how much pain does this cause directly... and what should our victims expect."

"I don't recall it hurting... though I was sick for the day after," I said.

"Really, well that's good and bad," said Sick. "Good in that I won't cause any more pain... bad in that the pain caused might have been unnecessary. I will ask my wife to send you something later. I will want your opinions on it, for official records."

Calamity nodded.

"Lastly, we are a bit busy to look into the whole missing Jay situation. Let us know if you hear or see anything."

CHAPTER 6

The following Friday I was looking at some data, and I had found the main discrepancy.

"The biggest difference," I began, "Is that the sample provided by Sick does not include sequence G143. In your notes, you said that G143 was a soothing agent?"

"Yes," said Calamity. "In previous studies with small arthropods, it seemed to greatly reduce the stress the organism was facing. Often from somewhat lethal to merely displaying symptoms of sickness for a short period of time."

"I also recall him asking me if transforming hurt… did he mean to ask that as a hypothetical… or as in… did he have reason to think it would?"

"I don't know… hold on." She pulled her phone out of her pocket; it was vibrating. "Well speak of the devil." She tapped the screen twice, "Hello officer Sick, you are on speaker don't say frick."

Sick laughed, "I won't then, I have a few questions… first off is Ms. Trixie Night there?"

"I am," I said, "Is Sue there?"

"Right… hold on let me get her," said Sick and a few moments later…

"Hello, what do you need me for?" asked Sue.

"I have to ask Trixie a question," said Sick. "This is for an official record so don't say frick."

"Understood," said Sue. "I will not say frick and I absolutely won't say count."

"So my plan is that I will ask a question to Ms. Night, if Sue objects, she should say so. Otherwise, and if you have no objections, please answer the question."

"I understand," I said.

"All clear on my end," said Sue.

"First off, for the official record, when you were accidentally transformed did you feel any pain?"

I gave Sue a second to object, she did not. "I don't recall being in pain."

"May I ask the same question about the transition back?"

"I felt… unwell afterward, but not in physical pain… more like a bad cold."

"I see… Finally, and this is open to Dr. Calamity as well, have either of you had time to examine the data I sent your way?"

"I was actually just done, and talking to Dr. Calamity about it," I said.

"She had just told me that the sample you gave us is missing one gene sequence that appears in our own mixture," said Calamity. "Sequence G143, which is meant to be a soothing agent… makes the process less stressful on the subject, and in some cases allows for it to be survived at all."

"I see," said Sick, "And you use this sequence in your samples?"

"Hold on," said Sue. "Dr. Calamity this question might be too much."

"My apologies," said Sick. "I am trying to ascertain if the original abductors… might have… skipped a vital step… I don't like human traffickers, and I especially don't like human traffickers that turn people into sheep. Which, by the way, we have confirmed now. Anyway… I wanted to see if they might have also been negligent in some way… a person from the ASPCA assessed the conditions and declared them unfit for sheep. So I figured why not double-check, and see if we can nail them with a few more laws."

"I see," said Sue. "But the answer could be incriminating if it fell into the wrong hands."

"How would it… oh… sorry," said Sick. "Perhaps we shouldn't do this over the phone."

The next day we came to Sick's office; he drove us there in his car. Sue was with us the entire time.

"So for the record, can you talk about the reason you used sequence G143?"

Calamity and Sue whispered quietly for a moment, and then Sue nodded.

"It was used for several reasons, survivability, and health, of the test subject. Its use was high on the list for both ethical and practical reasons."

"Good." said Sick, "Any other differences?"

Sue whispered into my ear, "What else did you find, before you tell him?"

"Nothing really," I whispered back.

"Ok, that should be fine to say," whispered Sue.

"That was the only major difference," I said.

"Would you care to speculate on its removal?" asked Sick. "What reason for not having it?"

I looked at Calamity who whispered with Sue. Calamity got a nod after the whispering.

"It is possible, but not confirmed to be true, that removing G143 might result in a cheaper treatment…but in previous studies, it had, in many cases, proven necessary for survival for most subjects."

Sick nodded, "I think that is all," he said. "Thank you for coming, let me take you two, and also my wife, to lunch as a thank you."

So he did, and he paid for it. It was a good lunch, and he drove us back to the lab, to find the door broken off its hinges.

"Wait here," said Sick getting his badge and gun; he got out of the car. "Dr. Calamity, do I have permission to enter the building?"

"Yes," she said.

Sick then walked in through the broken door, a minute later there was the sound of a scuffle, then Sue's phone rang.

"Yes dear?" she said. "Good… ohhh? Right… I will let them know…" She laughed for a minute, "Not this guy no, he will have to find some other lawyer." She turned to us, "Apparently he found the problem."

So we walked in and the lab was a mess, someone had scrummaged through the lab, paper was everywhere, the floor was covered in broken glass.

"Trixie can you please make sure that all hazardous materials are secure… if something is off let me know immediately," said Calamity.

"Yes ma'am," I said.

I checked the lab fridge. The bio and chem hazard containers there were still locked, as were the ones that did not require refrigeration. While checking these I heard shouting that sounded familiar.

"LET ME GO… I AM A FEDERAL AGENT," said a voice that sounded a lot like the Richard guy from… B.O.O.B?

"Where is your badge?" asked Sick.

"I DON'T HAVE IT ON ME," said the voice that sounded like Richard.

I saw that Calamity was near the shouting and went to her.

"All hazardous materials are secure," I said.

"Excellent," said Calamity. "We don't have to worry about this guy dying."

"That would have been a shame," said Sue. "This way I can squeeze this man for all he is worth."

"Is that the Richard guy from B.O.O.B.?" I asked Calamity.

"His name is Dick," said Calamity and Sue simultaneously.

"And Dick is under arrest," said Sick. "He has the right to remain silent, a right I wish he would express for my sake."

"UNHAND ME AT ONCE," said Dick.

"You know that when they say can and will be used against you. They mean can and absolutely WILL be used against you," said Sue. "Every sentence you utter gives me ammo."

Sue turned to us, "As soon as Sick's backup arrives we are going to catalog every bit of damage he has done to this place, make a full tally of everything that needs to be repaired or replaced. If your work has been interrupted or slowed give me a time estimate and cost in terms of salary and keeping the lab operational. When we go to court over this, and we will, we will have a cataloged cost of everything he owes us."

"YOU WON'T GET A CENT YOU COW!!!!" shouted Dick.

"Is that so?" said Sue looking at a security camera. "I wonder what that thing caught."

"I will go check the computer file," said Calamity.

"Not yet," said Sue. "Wait until the investigator arrives, then we will have someone to verify our version of events."

So we waited until the police showed up and we got to see on the recorded security footage Dick breaking in, and rummaging through everything, including killing every queen of Calamity's genetically modified bees.

"I had nearly completed an experiment with these guys, we were testing a species to make it more resilient to pollution and invasive bees. I was going to test them to see if it worked in practice in spring, now that's impossible. We have lost a year of work," said Calamity.

"We will get you compensated," said Sue.

"YOU CAN'T DO THIS TO ME, I AM A GOVERNMENT AGENT," shouted Dick.

"You have no badge, no warrant, no uniform," said one of Sick's officers. "Why do you expect me to believe you?"

"MY BOSS WILL MAKE YOU PAY FOR WHAT YOU HAVE DONE."

Dick was then dragged out, kicking and screaming the entire time. He managed to knock a cabinet door off its hinges, and knock over a sharp's waste receptacle.

"Everyone clear, I need to clean this up," said Calamity.

"Not yet," said Sick. "It's evidence. Let us take a sweep of this place, then clean it up."

"It was a container of used syringes and sharp objects. It's a potential biohazard."

"Our forensic team is used to biohazards. I will let them know beforehand to expect sharps on the floor."

The lab would be on lockdown for the next week. This made the university mad since five classes were scheduled to use it for the semester. Now no one can work here until it is cleaned and repaired. Dick had managed to damage some of the power and water lines. The eye wash station in the corner was out of order, as were some of the incubators… and the lab fridge. We had to relocate many sensitive materials to other fridges that now were filled to bursting and could not be used for their own labs. The bill to repair it was immense, and best of all, I was getting paid during all of this while doing nothing.

"Well," said Sick, "If you two are less busy, can I ask you to come in as outside experts some time …we found something… related to *Leaf it to Me?*"

A few days later, we stopped by Sue and Sick's place for that something. It was a pile of papers.

"These are some of the documents we found," said Sick. "The short version is that we know that they were working with others."

"Ok," said Calamity.

"And we think that they were outsourcing some of their material from others."

I nodded.

"But we don't know where they are."

"So why are you telling us?" asked Calamity.

"Because I am asking for your help finding the other sites," said Sick. "Our forensic team is one guy who is somewhat over-worked and he has threatened to quit unless we hire help. As far as my boss is concerned, he would rather spend the money trying to not lose the case they have against the fire department as badly as they already are, courtesy of my lovely wife.

"The short version is that one of the officers parked his cruiser in front of a fire hydrant," said Sue. "And the fire department needed that particular hydrant while the car was still there, so they broke the police cruiser to put out a fire." She smiled with a wicked smile. "The department just seems to want to make my job easier on this one."

Sick smiled, "As for the rest of the force," he said. "They won't help me anymore for some reason." He glanced at Sue with a smile, "And even if they did, the whole force has about one brain cell to share. It's not my turn to use that brain cell, so I have to ask you two for help.

"So in short, I have begged my boss to let you two take a look at this. I know it is a lot to ask, and of course the cheap bastard wouldn't free up a cent from the P-R budget, so I have to ask you to do this as volunteers. But well… as long as your lab is out of order, and I promise I can make it worth your while."

Sue spoke up, "Honey, are you getting corrupt on us?"

"No," said Sick. "But if ever you need the force to actually do its job, correctly, for once, I can force that issue through."

Sue nodded, I looked at Calamity.

"Well I can't promise anything," said Calamity. "But if Trixie or I have time, we may look over it."

"Thank you," said Sick, "That's really all I can ask."

CHAPTER 7

We started on the various files on *Leaf It to Me*. Each one was dryer and less readable than the last. I got to the point where I was aching for just something, anything interesting, in those damn files. One week of this and nothing interesting happened. Then Sue came to visit and we had a meeting about the various legal things we were now involved in.

"One last thing," she said, just after the second hour of an hour-long meeting. "I kind of want to see if Jay is connected to *Leaf It to Me* in any way."

I nodded, "That would make sense as I did see him in their parking lot."

Sue nodded, "But I mean, when he worked here, the mixture that turned you into a sheep came from Calamity. Could Jay have been using the same recipe?"

I looked to Calamity who looked just as stunned as I felt. "How did we not think of that?" she asked.

I shrugged, and I also saw Sue shrug. "It doesn't matter, we made the connection now. He is currently at large, could the recipe for the mixture that *Leaf It To Me* used, come from here?"

"No," said Calamity. "There were differences in the mixture, the treatment; Trixie found that it was missing something."

"Something that came with the recipe automatically, or something you had to add?"

Calamity blinked a few times, "Not really that simple, but

closer to being added."

"What specifically?"

"Sequence G143, it makes the experiences less traumatic for the organism experiencing it."

"In your judgment is this sequence necessary, or helpful."

"I have never done any transformation without it in the treatment, nor have I heard of any scientist anywhere working without it with any animal."

"What about non-animals."

"Usually recommended; some plants have survived without it, but have ended up sick afterwards."

"So it is entirely possible, that Jay took some of the mixtures, without G143, or the recipe and skipped that step, and used that to work on the sheep?"

Calamity blinked a few times, "Yes."

Sue then turned to me, "And we know, especially based on your experience there, that *Leaf It To Me* has stolen these kind of things in the past."

I shrugged, "Yes, as far as I am aware."

"Then as far as we are aware, could Jay have stolen the recipe, and skipped some of the steps, with G143 being the part that he skipped for time?"

"Honestly I think we might be overestimating him," I said. "He was never that good. It feels like a bit much for him to have found the recipe, read it, understood it enough to replicate it, and to see G143 as 'Optional' even though it really isn't. He could barely feed the lab mice without supervision."

Calamity nodded, "He was barely lab safe on a good day. One of us had to supervise him or he would do something stupid. The only thing he was good at was... Oh"

"Oh, what?"

"He did some of my gene mixes, and the day he got fired…
he was messing with it in the food safe fridge."

"The same mix that got Trixie?" Sue raised an eyebrow.

Calamity nodded.

"Was this the first time he had his hands on the mixture?"

"No?"

"Because I looked over your records, and he was around
when you started working with that transformation into sheep
mix, *Leaf It To Me* started having Sapi sheep later that same
week."

I looked to Calamity, who was blinking quite a bit.

"Let me get my records," she finally said before standing up.

Sue turned to me, "What about you? Did you notice
anything?"

"I don't remember anything from then," I said. "Just that
he stared at my breasts all day, I started wearing baggy clothes
to keep his eyes away from me."

Sue nodded, "And you complained to HR about that, which
is a whole other deal. Good news on that; they have sent out a
few feelers for settlement. Given the state of this whole mess,
and also the email his dad sent you, I think we could get you a
solid half a mill if we settled now."

"That might be nice," I said.

"I will let you think on that for now. Calamity, good to see
you and your laptop."

"Let me look through my records," said Calamity. "I might
have some old emails on that."

We waited for about a minute. Then Calamity's jaw seemed
to drop.

"Oh my god."

"What is it Calamity?" asked Sue.

Calamity turned her laptop around and showed Sue without saying a word.

Sue stared at the screen for a few seconds.

"I caught Mr. Walker playing with some solution that is part of my transformation experiments. It is meant to be able to turn a roughly sheep-sized animal into a sheep. In theory, it might work on humans as well. Despite this and when I told him to stop, he got confrontational, and shouted "You're not the boss of me." While this is just his first day, it shows that he has no idea how to work in a lab, or with others. I would like him to be moved to a different position if possible."

Sue blinked, "You have this dated, and the response shows that the message was heard. Trixie as your lawyer do not take the half a million, I would wait, we could get you so much more."

"Because it means he worked with *Leaf It To Me?*" I asked.

"Not really proof of that, but it was not part of what they disclosed to me, which makes their position worse."

"Sorry I didn't see that sooner," said Calamity.

"It's alright," said Sue. "We are still in discovery."

Then Sue's cell phone went off. "One sec, Yes Dear… Really? OK we are on our way."

Calamity looked at Sue who started to stand up.

"My husband thinks they found something. He wants you two there to help"

So we piled out into Sue's car, and were off to wherever Sick had sent us. It was a half hour drive to another town, with, among other things, an old abandoned bar. Inside that bar was a bunch of trash. After three hours all the trash had been searched and we found… nothing.

Half an hour later, Sick who looked somewhere between

mad and furious, came to us with another officer, head looking down, in tow.

"This is officer Bull Lee," said Sick. "Lee would you like to tell these three lovely ladies, one of whom is a lawyer and also my wife, why they are here."

Lee glanced up briefly, then back down, "Because you asked them to be here?"

Sick seemed to pause for a moment, "That is technically correct, but while others might call that the best kind of correct, it misses an important detail."

"Which is Sir?"

"Why did I call them here."

"Because you thought we had something."

"Why did I think we had something?"

"Because I told you… Sir."

"What did you tell me?"

"That one of the guys we had arrested told us that this was part of their operations… sir"

"When did they do that?"

"During interrogation sir."

"What techniques did you use."

"I… intimidated the suspect sir."

"Why did you do that?"

"Because I thought it would work sir."

"Why did you think it would work?"

"Because… because it worked on TV sir."

At that point I glanced at Sue and Calamity, both of whom were shaking their heads. Sue was pinching her nose and let out a sigh.

Sick continued, "Was the information actually good?"

"No sir," said Lee.

"Why do you think that?"

"Perhaps the suspect made something up sir?"

"Wow this one figured it out fast," said Sick clapping slowly, "I am almost impressed. Tell me when did you have that revelation?"

"When we didn't find anything sir."

"So you didn't think about the possibility of a suspect lying?"

"… No sir. I thought he couldn't lie under pressure."

"Does it sound stupid now that you said it out loud?"

"Yes sir."

"So, summarize what you have done."

"I have wasted several hours of everyone's time, and possibly made any results from interrogating that witness worthless legally and practically."

"Yes… but you have done enough for today. Luckily for you the only thing I can do is suspend you without pay. Unluckily for you, Judge Lou Phol, will be the judge when we decide whether or not to fire you."

Officer Lee gulped, "Is that the judge that got the officer who searched a car without permission fired?"

"Yes it is… Bull, you are correct."

Bull Lee gulped again and walked away.

Sick softened his gaze, "Sorry, you came out all this way for nothing."

CHAPTER 8

The next few weeks were slow. The only notable thing was somehow, Dick from B.O.O.B. got out of jail. Sue was happy though, and given that the lab was going to be rebuilt from scratch, with an air conditioner and new everything by the end of the semester was exciting. Suspiciously this was agreed around the time that Dick from B.O.O.B. got out of jail, and around the time I also got a rather generous check from the "Bureau of Odd Biology."

In the meantime, Sick had me looking over anything they could get from *Leaf it to Me*. We looked through everything and found little. So time for a meeting on how we have nothing.

"So we have nothing on our end," said Calamity. "How about you?"

"I wish I could say we had nothing," said Sick. "It would imply we had more than we actually do. What I have is a dozen false leads, a mayor breathing down my neck to catch speeders, over-eager officers who keep trying to do dumb stuff, and a lawyer telling me that because some over-eager officer did dumb stuff I have evidence to throw out. Not that it was helping much anyway."

"Is there any good news?" asked Sue.

"A question about how what kind of resources would be required to run that place. Most of the suspects claim they made the solution themselves, but a few say it was imported. Dr. Calamity can you help determine what they would need to make that gene solution, bare minimum?

Calamity looked at me, "Trixie that will be your job for the next while."

I got started on that the next day. I decided that I wanted to start by replicating Calamity's method and then try to modify it down to the bare minimum. I couldn't use animals for this because… ethics; flowers would have to do.

The first time, I did a simple dandelion to clover transformation, they were cheap and fairly close to what I needed to emulate. After making sure I could do it, I started experimenting. Keeping one standard batch, and then removing one step of the preparation process. I was able to do an experiment every other day this way. Finally, after a month, I got down to the minimum where the dandelions transformed, though about half died.

"That checks out with what we saw," said Sick, "based on what our victims estimated."

"Can you do an experiment on live animals to be sure?"

"That will be difficult," I said. "I used plants because of ethical reasons, to use animals I have to go by the ethics board, and they probably won't like it."

"Why?"

"Because many of the steps are meant to stop undo stress on the organism. If we did this…"

"I can do it," said Calamity. "I can convince the board to approve of it."

Sue looked around then to Calamity, "How?"

"By telling them the truth," said Calamity. "I will tell them why this is important." She turned to Sick, "So I need to know exactly what you are planning."

Sick sighed, then looked down for a moment before returning his gaze to calamity "If we know the minimum that they used we can look for anyone who ordered just those parts. I don't think I will completely make it easy, but it might narrow it down."

Before that could happen, a certain Dick from B.O.O.B demanded an interview.

When Dick saw that I brought Sue with me, he shook his head.

"A lawyer, you know that you only need a lawyer if you're feeling guilty," he said.

"Or if you don't trust the police to be one hundred percent benevolent one hundred percent of the time," said Sue.

"How cynical do you have to be to think that?" said Dick.

"Not cynical," said Sue. "I just believe that a system has to include a way to correct itself to prevent abuse or mistakes. That is my job, I make sure that no one else who is doing their job, takes it too far."

"And what if you represent a guilty client? One who you knew was guilty?"

"Someone has to… someone has to see that you don't take it too far in your pursuit of justice. Someone has to speak up for even the vilest so we don't use excuses to go too far."

Dick stood up and smiled, "And what if you got, say a murderer, free on a technicality?"

"Like what? What kind of technicality?" asked Sue with a raised eyebrow.

"Say the search warrant wasn't properly filed and the incriminating evidence had to be thrown out? You made that argument, then the killer walks free, how do you sleep at night?" Dick had the smile of a man who thought he had caught his prey.

Sue tilted her head and spoke. "I would take comfort in the fact that every time, from then on, that the rookies in training were being told about getting and properly executing warrants, this story would be told. That the next ten generations of cops would have it drilled into them that they have to do the whole thing properly. And that because of that, every young fool who thinks it's good enough that they meant well, will stop and get a warrant. And because of that, there will be an opportunity to find, and correct mistakes before they affect a real person's life."

"The young rookie got the warrant properly, thus a judge looked over the evidence thus far, spotted a mistake, and told the rookie about said mistake. The rookie starts over, this time getting a new result, the actual perpetrator, and not an innocent. This one killer got away, but a hundred innocents did not have cops bust down their door, were not falsely accused, and were not blamed while the real killer got away to kill again. If that's the trade that I have to make, I will sleep very soundly."

Dick's jaw hung loosely from his face. "Well… um…" he stammered, "That one killer could kill… again."

Sue nodded, "And another hundred will be caught before they can kill again, with a hundred innocents living life unbothered, because we have a way to double-check."

The look on Dick's face reminded me of deer in headlights.

"My turn," said Sue, as Dick went from deer in headlights to mouse facing down a particularly sadistic cat.

"How did you make bail?" asked Sue.

"My boss," said Dick. "He got the money… and he's… not happy."

"Did he say why?" asked Sue.

Dick stammered for a moment, "Something about his boss being upset."

"So you didn't pay attention?"

"He was always whining about something, getting in my way, like you."

"You tried to arrest Dr. Calamity for not giving you photos of Bigfoot that she literally did not have."

"I know she has them; I can feel it in my gut."

"Your gut is wrong, and if you have nothing intelligent to say to me or Trixie, we will be leaving."

"You can't…"

"Sure we can, unless you have something to arrest us on." She turned to me, "Let's go."

We got up and started toward the door.

Dick's shoulders shook, "Wait."

Sue turned to look at him, "If you have something to say, say it and stop wasting my time… now."

Dick was sweating bullets, despite the office being air conditioned to within an inch of its life. "I need to know how you got that formula, for the morphing of animals and stuff."

Sue looked to me and nodded.

"Calamity got it from another scientist," I said, "Someone else working with genetics."

"Who?" asked Sue.

"Some guy called Doctor Bizarre," I said.

Sue turned to glare at Dick, "Well."

Dick looked like a deer caught in the headlights. "That… how… How did this Bizarre get it?"

"Doctor Bizarre," said Sue before turning to me, "Did Calamity say?"

"She said that Dr. Bizarre had developed it," I said, "Or at least refined it from single to multi-celled organisms. People have been working on this stuff for a while."

"How long?" demanded Dick, "Answer Me."

Sue held her hand out as a cue for me to stay silent, and turned to Dick, "What's the magic word?"

Dick blinked, "What?"

"You know, like your mom taught you, when you were a little boy and wanted something from mommy, or a teacher, or a relative, what did she teach you to say?"

Dick laughed, "You can't be serious."

Sue said nothing, just stared him down.

He turned to me "I am a federal agent; you will answer my question."

I said nothing and waited for Sue to signal me, she continued to stare Dick down.

"This is ridiculous," he said.

He glanced around the room, then looked down and quietly mumbled something.

"I'm sorry, but I couldn't hear that, could you say it again louder?"

Dick glanced up. "Please," he said in a barely audible whisper.

"Louder" said Sue.

Dick sighed, "Please, would you tell me how long people have been working on this, please?"

Sue looked to me and nodded.

"I can't say for sure," I said, "But it's been a while, a decade at least, probably more, I remember a documentary on it when I was a kid."

I saw a look of shock and then panic spread across Dicks face. "You're free to go," he said before running out of the room.

We were out of there a moment later. "Ah Dick from Boob," I said, "It feels like all his problems could be solved by a simple internet search."

"I think he is after you because he thinks you're as guilty as Calamity," said Sue. "You work for her, in his mind that means you know what she knows, and probably sees this as a humiliation he can't stand." She patted me on the shoulder, "Be careful, he may be an idiot, but he is an idiot of the government."

After a few more weeks Calamity was done with her experiments. She gave Sick a short list of steps, and thus equipment, that the process might work with. Sick took that and started narrowing down the search.

I was busy with classes but still made time to settle out of court with the school. Basically, they canceled out the rest of my tuition and paid back what had been spent on them. Calamity made some noise of not being done, apparently, with the school. We still had to take on Papa Walker.

Speaking of which, he was still out there, somewhere. In other news I needed to buy groceries and spent some time on my least busy non-weekend day, Thursday. I had only gotten the bare essentials, coffee, ice cream, chocolate, potato chips and donuts. I also treated myself and grabbed a pre-made salad. I had just loaded up into Hank's trunk, my car, remember, and then I found myself staring down Jay. He was standing across the lane in the parking lot, glaring at me.

I stepped back to get into Hank and drive away.

"Where do you think you're going B***," said Jay. "Too afraid." He started to walk toward me, "You think you're so special, you ruined my life." He licked his lips, "I want something, something from you." He grinned evilly.

I stood by my door, wondering if I should run, shout for help, or try to get into Hank, lock the door, and drive away.

Jay stepped forward, "I am going to…" He didn't get to finish that sentence, as he got hit by some idiot in a pickup truck that I distinctly remember had only one bag of groceries in its giant truck bed. The pickup then backed up, turned, and quickly drove around Jay, smashing into another car's tail lights on the way out of the parking lot.

I debated calling Sick or calling 911, I decided it would probably be better to call 911 and noticed the phone already in my hand. I dialed 911 and waited for the operator to pick up. Instead, I got hold music.

"You have reached the Dedlam emergency assistance office," said an automated voice after 30 seconds, "Your emergency is important to us, please continue to hold."

Apparently, my emergency was not important enough to answer on the one line that probably should never have hold music. The music continued for another minute, then finally the operator answered.

"Sorry about that," said the operator. She sighed, "Another old woman complaining about young people having a picnic, anyway, 911 what's your emergency?"

"A guy who I used to work with, who sort of slightly harassed me, and is wanted by the police on completely unrelated charges, that I am also involved with, has just been run over by a pickup truck."

"Did the pickup truck stay there?"

"No they ran off immediately."

"Ok, sending an ambulance to your location… who got hit?"

"Jay Walker."

"You mean Mister Jay Walker?"

"Yes."

"There is an outstanding warrant for his arrest, I will send a squad car."

Both showed up quickly, though the police car smashed the same car that the pickup smashed on the way out. Now it was smashed on both sides.

The paramedics loaded Jay into the ambulance.

"Do you have insurance?" asked the medic.

Jay cried slightly and gave the medic his wallet; the medic looked in it and found the insurance card.

Meanwhile, a second cop car arrived, this one had Sick in it.

"OK change of plans, can you make the arrest?" he asked the other cop. They nodded.

"OK, I will talk to the witness."

The second cop sighed, "The one time I get to make an arrest and he's already secured in the back of a stretcher."

Sick walked up to me. "Trixie how are you doing?" he asked.

"Could be worse," I said, "But now my ice cream is going to melt."

Sick nodded, "Honestly I would like to let you go and save it, but I have to go through a whole witness interview process."

We went through the whole process and sure enough, my ice cream melted. By this time the manager of the store had come out to see what was going on. So I opened up Hank's trunk to throw the melted stuff out and get new ice cream.

"All melted?" said the manager.

"Yeah," I said, "I guess I have to get new stuff; I don't think it will re-freeze."

"Probably not," said the manager. "I can get you some new ones."

"Thank you," I said.

He was back in five minutes with fresh ice cream, and an angry lady following him.

"Why are you helping her? You should be helping me, my ice cream melted too, get me new ice cream," the woman said.

"Ma-am," said the manager, "Her ice-cream melted because she had to talk to the police officer, your ice cream melted because you spent twenty minutes yelling at an employee for something that was not his fault. I am understaffed, and people like you are not helping. Besides, she was polite about it."

The manager loaded up Hank with ice cream. More than I had originally purchased.

"It's on the house," said the manager.

"Thank you," I said.

"No problem," said the manager, who then walked off, the angry woman shouting at him the whole way.

CHAPTER 9

I was given another task, to speak to a guy whom Jay mentioned while being interrogated in his hospital bed. Now I was in a van traveling toward… somewhere.

"I will be watching the entire time," said Sick. "We will have a microphone listening and if you need help, the code word is antidisestablishmentarianism."

I gave Sick a stink eye.

"Look, it's not likely to come up in conversation," he said. "That way you won't accidentally say it, right."

I nodded, "I suppose."

Sick nodded too, "The goal is for you to speak about the therapy. We have presented you as a potential buyer."

"Right," I said, "We talked about this."

"Just going over everything before we send you in." Sick started pacing, "One last little thing, while we are here if you need help, we don't want to jump in unless we have to. So try not to aggravate the situation."

"So, the code word is antidisestablishmentarianism, pretend to be a buyer, don't aggravate the situation, got it."

"One last thing," said Sick, handing me something. "An earpiece, have it in an ear and we will be able to talk to you."

Sick nodded, "Good luck."

The van pulled up by a… run down… probably abandoned… building, I got out of the van and walked to the building. The smell of cigarette smoke choked me, and it looked like the building was once a bar or restaurant, but hadn't been for a while.

"To make sure you can hear us and we can hear you… say, I don't know, 'nice place'".

"Nice place," I said.

"Ok, we can hear you," said Sick. "And you can hear us."

I then saw the contact. She was a… not horribly attractive-looking woman middle-aged, smoking, and appearing to need a bit of exercise. If the term "White Trash" had a face, it was hers.

"Ms. Banks?" I asked.

"My name is Robbin," said the woman in a voice that sounded like an old beat-up car trying to start. "You must be Trixie?"

I nodded, and Robbin gestured toward a seat across from what was once a restaurant booth.

"Have a seat."

I sat down trying not to gag on the smell of cigarettes and hoping that there was not tetanus in my seat.

"Tell me Trixie," said Robbin. "What is your take on antidisestablishmentarianism?"

"Uh-oh," said Sick in my ear.

"I can't say I have heard of it," I said hoping she couldn't see the earpiece or any wires from the… wire I was wearing.

"Just act natural," said Sick in my ear.

"It's an idea," said Robbin. "That we shouldn't decouple church and state."

"I can't say I am for it," I said. "After all if anyone should be worried about the government, it should be people like me."

"Disappointing," said Robbin. "I am very much for antidisestablishmentarianism, think about it, if the police aren't too busy arresting atheists, could they come after us?"

I shrugged, "I never thought of it that way."

Robbin smiled, "Good, now let's talk business."

"Yeah," I said, "I have heard that you have some sort of transformation serum."

Robbin nodded, "And our previous customer recently got shut down, so before we go any further, are you a cop, or working with one, because if you are, you can't lie?"

"Yes, you can lie," said Sick in my ear. "I have no idea why people think that."

"I am not with the cops," I said, lying.

"Good," said Robbin. "Now, this serum can turn a person into a sheep, what would you do with this if I gave it to you?"

"I can't say," I said. "All I know is that my client wants the serum, and is willing to pay for it. If it can do what you say it can."

Sick's voice, filtered into my ear, "Good job so far."

"Well," said Robbin, "I am hoping you won't get the idea to use these as part of a petting zoo. Our previous customers got shut down because they thought they could use the sheep as show animals, perfectly trained, ha. So, before I sell this to you, what are you going to do with it?"

"We both know that you don't have many customers," I said.

"You may be right," said Robbin. "But… How did you know?"

"I do now," I said.

Robbin cursed herself quietly for about a minute.

"Fine… as per your request I can give you a sample," said Robbin holding up a small vial. "Not much, just barely enough for one treatment, you want any more, you call me."

I nodded, "Of course," I said before walking out of the building and back to the van.

I handed the sample to Sick who put the sample on ice. "Jeeves, home please," said Sick.

"You got it, boss," said the guy in the driver's seat.

We arrived back without incident. From there everything went quiet for a week then it was time for a meeting. Sick, Calamity, Sue, and I were all there along with many police officers.

Sick started the presentation holding a laser pointer and slide changer in his hand. "So far thanks to a plea deal from Mr. Jay Walker we were able to find Ms. Robbin Banks, who got us a sample of the agent that *Leaf It To Me* used to turn people into sheep. With that… Mr. Decops…"

One police officer, who was snoozing, suddenly sat upright.

"Pay attention," said Sick glaring at the officer. "Or I might have to drum you back to dispatch, Collin."

There were a few laughs at Collin's expense.

"Right," said Sick, turning back to the projected PowerPoint. "With Dr. Calamity's help we identified one thousand seven hundred and eighty-three labs that might have had the equipment to do this." The slide showed a map of the U.S with many red dots. "Based on what she found in the sample, she was then able to reduce it to thirty-two." The slide changed to the same map with fewer dots, "Of those, twenty-one were all above board, leaving just eleven." This last slide showed just that. "Calamity has also told us that Ms. Trixie Night knows the next piece of the puzzle pretty well."

Now it was my turn. I got up to do my portion of the presentation. Sick handed me the pointer and I forwarded the presentation. My first slide showed a map of the Tennessee and North Carolina border with a small marker on one region, a bright orange beetle-like insect with a big jaw, and a plant that reached about ankle height on a person's foot right next to it, with a small square blue flower at the top of its stalk.

"This," I said, pointing to the flower with a laser pointer on my remote, "Is *Rose transfigurator*. It is a small plant about four inches or ten centimeters in height. The locals call it bug weed." I moved the pointer to the insect, "This beetle-looking thing is called *Mutata arthropodibus*. Locals call it weed bug. It is a small venomous beetle-like insect, it is carnivorous, and they tend to be located near bug weeds. Both organisms are found here," I said, lasering the marker on the map. "Near Marks Knob, a mountain just barely in the North Carolina side of the Great Smoky Mountains. Additionally, weed bugs have never been observed mating, laying eggs, or having any sort of larva. Turns out there is a reason for that."

I moved forward one slide with a video. Starting the video, we saw a grasshopper land on and start eating a leaf of bug weed. Then a little fast-forward marker in the corner let us know the footage was sped up in a time lapse. The grasshopper then fell off the leaf, started convulsing, then its exoskeleton, its body, split open for a weed bug to crawl out of it. The video then ended and went back to the beginning.

I turned to the room full of stunned faces, or maybe they were asleep, I couldn't tell.

"May I ask… what was that?" said Sick.

I wasn't sure whether he was curious or trying to get the other cops to pay attention. "That was a grasshopper turning into a weed bug," I said. "The natural defense of bug weed is a fluid that it produces that… well… does that. The new weed bug will not only eat any other insect trying to eat a bug weed but will also aggressively attack larger animals that come near the plant… to a point.

"People have been working on this for a while. When all of this was first discovered scientists quickly started researching it to see what could be done with this discovery. The result was the first transformation serum. Thus far researchers have not been able to replicate the abilities of bug weed, without ground-up bug weed. Somewhat inconveniently, the plant also doesn't take well to captivity. My thesis is actually on doing just that, getting bug weed to like captivity and being farmed."

"Miss," said the officer Sick scolded earlier, Collin. "Two things, one, did getting it to grow in captivity work, and two, if I eat it… what would happen to me, would I turn into a bug?"

"So for your first question, sort of," I said. "For the second question, vertebrates seem to be immune unless the material made by bug weed is extensively processed."

Calamity spoke up for a moment, "That has largely been my work."

Calamity gestured for me to continue and I did so. "Anyway, bug weed doesn't like captivity, and if you want a transformation serum you will need some material from the plants. Marks Knob is now basically crawling with forestry service and park rangers who try to limit who has access to the plants. They even fenced off some areas, in order to protect the plant for research purposes. I doubt any criminal organization, especially one that is cheeping out on the treatment, has the capacity to raise these in captivity. Especially as how to raise the plants in captivity at all is an… ongoing question."

Sick raised his hand and I pointed to him.

"So if we can find out which one of the suspected labs from earlier was getting it, if we could track down which one of the eleven labs from before got their hands on bug weed, we could potentially find the source of what *Leaf It To Me* was using."

I nodded.

"The plant is protected and the forestry service is making a point of not letting too many plants get harvested at any one time," I said. "If we can work with them with our suspicions, we might be able to find the source."

Sick nodded, "I like this plan, any objections?"

No one said anything.

"Ok, then on with the presentation," he said standing up. I handed the pointer back to him and sat down.

"So," began Sick, "We know of an ingredient that our suspects need, we know where it is, and Calamity has confirmed that they are using it." He looked toward Calamity.

"There are some protein markers from bug weed in the solution Trixie retrieved," said Calamity.

Sick nodded, "So, if they have to get to Marks Knob, then we should keep a look out there. In a rather convenient twist, Trixie was already planning on going there over winter, and I have spoken to park rangers in the area, so we hope to have some eyes on the ground soon. Until then we will keep our eyes open for any happenings here."

CHAPTER 10

Months passed and winter arrived. I was only going to be near Marks Knob for a few weeks, in a town called Marks Jewels just to the south. It was a small town, a brand new town, based around bug weed. Everything was new, and it looked it as well. After seeing dozens of run-down wide spots in the road along the way, it was refreshing to see a brand new, modern and well-kept wide spot in the road.

It was a snowy winter, but I was used to driving in snow and Hank may be many things, but unable to handle snow he is not, especially if you know what you're doing.

I had an apartment here for one month, it was not a large apartment, one room, with an attached kitchen area, with a fridge/freezer, oven, dishwasher, and kitchen sink. Next to the bed was a closet with a washer and dryer with a place for clean clothes hanging right next to it.

After getting unpacked, for the most part, I decided to get something to eat. The town was walkable, and since traffic was crazy, I went for a walk in the cold. I found a sandwich place, Deliciously Long, a chain restaurant, but one I knew was good. It was clean, wood floors, living room-style atmosphere, and smelled like fresh bread.

I had a sailor's sub, which was big, long, and full of meat. Then I had a call with Ranger Ford Solo.

"Hello Trixie," said Ford in a voice that gave the image of a handsome man. "I take it you just got here."

"Yes," I said, "Nice to hear from you Ranger Ford Solo."

"Well… first off, you can call me Ford," he said. "I am looking forward to this, lots of good work from your mentor, Dr. Calamity. If you have a hundredth of her skill you will be a huge boon to us. But I also hear you are connected to a police investigation."

I nodded, before remembering I was making a phone call. "Yes, someone is misusing the treatments made by *Rose transfigurator*."

"Just call it bug weed, and I had heard about that. Some small farm thing in Montana."

"Yeah, the police don't think that they could have made it themselves without help, we need to figure out where it was made."

Ford sighed, "That will make everything more difficult, you don't have too much on your plate do you?"

"Honestly I could use a break, but I think I am OK for now," I said.

Ford was silent for a moment. "Sorry, forgot you can't hear me nod," he said. "Anyway, I would recommend that you just focus on taking your pictures and making your measurements. And if you happen to see something for the police let them know. I have ramped up patrols, but most of the guys are going on Christmas break soon. So it will be just us. When you come in tomorrow, I want to speak to you about this in private, there is something you should know."

"Can't we talk about it now?"

"No not really."

I sighed, "See you tomorrow."

The next day I travelled to Ranger Ford's office. It was actually inside a small but well-kept museum that seemed to be attached to the park/national forest. There were exhibits on everything from The Tragedy of the Commons, which is an overuse issue of shared space/resources, to pictures of some of the plants and animals you might find active at various times of the year there. A few live snakes, lizards, salamanders, forest mice, some fish. And of course a small exhibit on bug weed, its effects, and how we might put it to work helping humans. Not much of that mattered to me initially. I needed to talk to Ranger Ford.

I saw that he was in a meeting with someone, with a familiar voice… it was Dick, from B.O.O.B.

"Mr. Ford," said Dick. "I would appreciate you calling me Richard."

"And I would appreciate you trying to understand that I am not making everything up just to annoy you," said Ford. "I cannot give you what you are asking for, not without a warrant."

Ford was sitting down, looked unamused at Dick who, even from behind was visibly fuming. Ford seemed calm, and was, as I expected, very handsome, appeared to be tall even sitting down, with dark hair, a trimmed beard and was wearing a park ranger uniform.

Dick scratched his chin, "But you could… say… leave copies of the photos on your desk, step out to get coffee and if I happen to have found what I need in that time we could forgo all of this," he said.

Ford shook his head, "Sorry Dick, that sounds like a way to end my career here very quickly, I would have to actually like you, at least a little, to stick my neck out that far."

Dick growled at Ford.

"If you are convinced that one of my camera traps happened to catch a photo of Bigfoot, why not get your own and put them out," said Ford with a smug smile.

Dick growled at Ford, "I did, and I got nothing."

Ford tilted his head, "Then maybe I also don't have that picture either. Have you considered that?"

Even from behind I could tell Dick was glaring at Ford.

"Now if you will excuse me," said Ford. "Someone who actually scheduled a meeting with me is behind you and I can't keep her waiting.

Dick turned around and looked at me with a face I can only describe as absolute contempt.

I waved at Dick, "Hello, fancy seeing you here."

Dick walked toward me, "What are you doing here."

"You should know that Sue, my lawyer, gave me a number to call if you ever bothered me again. Do you want me to pull it up?"

Dick grunted and began storming out.

"I take it you have had the displeasure of meeting everyone's least favorite government agent," said Ford.

I nodded, "He is quite special."

Ford laughed, "Have a seat, close the door behind you." He looked behind me and spoke a bit louder. "I would like to show you the photos that a certain Dick wanted to see. Given your situation, I can share them with you Trixie."

I stepped into Ford's office, looked behind me to see Dick fuming, and closed the door behind me.

Ford's office seemed like a mess. Folders piled on top of each other, pencils strewn everywhere, papers piled up in messy piles that looked almost ready to fall over. For his part Ford quickly dug through one of the piles and plucked from it, seemingly without looking, a booklet of photographs, the first one visible from the top, looked like Ford in a forest taken from below.

"This is what I couldn't tell you about last night," said Ford putting the booklet of photos in front of me. "Camera traps, we place them nearby anywhere bug weed grows, between its potential for misuse and scarcity, we have to keep an eye on the stuff we have."

I began looking through the photos, most of them were of deer, raccoons, the occasional bear or coyote. And a few humans, most of whom appeared to be hunters, hikers, campers, or other outdoorsmen; only one appeared to notice the plant. In the photo time stamped for immediately after that viewer, the bug weed was gone. Sadly, the face of the person in the photo was obscured.

"So you see the issue," Ford said.

"Yeah someone grabbed a bug weed plant," I said "Not great."

Ford nodded, "Obviously I can't let you walk out with that, the locations of these plants is a carefully guarded secret, and for very good reason. We don't want bug weed going extinct or being misused, and I can only show you this because you signed a non-disclosures agreement. I was hoping you would recognize that person, from your separate investigation."

I shook my head, "Doesn't ring a bell, sorry."

Ford sighed, "I was afraid of that. Still, you have your own work to do. Finding out what is different from the bug weed you tried to grow in captivity, versus the stuff we find here."

"You mean aside from the fact that mine all died within a month?"

"Don't be so negative, they sprouted, and grew for a bit, correct? As far as I know, very few people have gotten even that far. And if we could grow bug weed in a greenhouse, or even in the field, we could keep a better eye on it, be less concerned about extinction of the plant and this whole area could be fully cordoned off to hopefully prevent misuse."

I nodded, "I know the whole spiel."

Ford nodded, "They are very picky plants, only grow here in the wild, and don't like other places, especially in captivity. In short, even four of the fifty seeds we sent you sprouting is something of a miracle."

I furrowed my brow, "Fifty? I only received ten."

Ford blinked, "Are you sure?"

"I can double-check the paperwork but I received ten seeds, I am sure."

"How many did you order?"

"Ten."

Ford pulled a file out of the pile on his desk and opened it up.

"We got a manifest and payment for fifty… if what you are saying is true… then we have a problem."

CHAPTER 11

Ford and I were suddenly spending the day going through paperwork. It was supposed to be a relatively short day, just taking some measurements to compare with what I already had. Now instead we were looking through piles of piles of papers, WORD docs, PDFs, anything that might hold some info on what happened.

What we found out quickly was that the paperwork was correct, mostly. Everything Ford had received was for fifty plants, and he sent fifty. Everything I had sent was for ten seeds, and I had ten. So somewhere in between someone was intercepting the papers and changing the numbers, and taking forty plant seeds with them.

"Ok," said Ford, "Let's think about how this could disappear. Is there anyone else who might have had a chance to interfere?"

"The Bureau Of Odd Biology," I said. "I sent the request through them."

"And I sent the seeds through them… every seed or plant I have sent was sent through them," said Ford.

We looked at each other and Ford started digging through a filing cabinet, then he picked up a phone and started talking to the person on the other end.

"Hi it's Ford… listen I just wanted to double-check how many plants you received… all twenty… OK good… no don't worry about it, yes… if there is a problem I will let you know."

Ford put the phone down. "I sent him fifty as well; someone is intercepting them. If its someone in B.O.O.B.... We need a lawyer."

I nodded, "Give me a second." I got my cell phone out and called Sue. "Hi Sue."

"Hey Trixie," said Sue. "Did you find something, get in trouble or just want to talk?"

"Found something."

"Oh good, I might get paid for that; my husband's new boat won't pay for itself."

"There seems to be a discrepancy between what Ford here at Marks Knob is sending out and what people are asking for. All of his paperwork checks out except for the numbers... he thinks that someone is interfering between us and them. And that that someone is part of the Bureau Of Odd Biology."

"I see," said Sue. "We will need to do something about that... I will book a flight and head over there, see you tomorrow probably."

"Ok thanks," I said.

Sue hung up and I turned to Ford. "The lawyer is on her way, familiar with this sort of stuff, and probably in it for more than just money."

Ford smiled and nodded. "That only leaves one question for today. How many samples do you want for your project?"

Ford selected ten samples. I began the process of comparing the ten wild samples to my ten "lab-raised" samples. My goal was to use the wild samples as a control to my lab-grown samples. Unfortunately, mine all died long ago but maybe it would get someone closer to growing bug weed in captivity.

Sue arrived the next day and spent most of it in her hotel making phone calls while I worked with Ford on my project. However, Sue did ask to have a meeting at the end of the day.

"So I have contacted some of the labs that Ford sent samples to. Asked for copies of the paperwork related to bug weed samples. Got a few responses and here is what I know. At least eight other labs, everyone that called me back, made smaller requests than the paperwork Ford received. All other paperwork checks out on both ends, so someone doctors the paperwork to change the number of samples requested."

"So why the discrepancy?" asked Ford.

"That is the question of the hour," said Sue. "I have two guesses, one, is that it is happening here and someone here is doctoring and stealing extra samples. The other is that there is a middleman, the Bureau Of Odd Biology.

"Have you heard of… Dick from B.O.O.B.?" asked Ford.

Sue nodded, "Do you think he had something to do with it?"

"Well he was here yesterday; tried to investigate without a warrant."

Sue smiled at Ford, "Either he suspects you, in which case you need a lawyer, or he is trying to cover his tracks. In that case you should prosecute, and you will need a lawyer."

Ford sighed, "How much will this cost me?"

"If I am bad, a lot. If I am good, not a cent… But I am very good. I will do some more work tomorrow. I think I can schedule a meeting with someone for tomorrow.

The next day Sue got us a video call with Gerald Mann, a middle-aged to older man with frazzled grey hairs, messy half-shaven beard, and a suit that almost looked nice. In general, he looked like the sort of man who could benefit from a few months of vacation literally anywhere. He was the head of the Bureau Of Odd Biology. Sue hoped we could get some answers from him, but getting anything from a G-Man would be hard at the best of times.

"So," said Gerald, who looked like he needed a vacation years ago. "I hear you have an issue… what is it? Does it involve Dick?"

"We don't know for sure if it involves Dick," said Sue. "But we think that someone in your organization might be doctoring documents to steal bug weed."

Gerald peered through the screen for a moment and blinked a few times. "Excuse me for a moment." He got up and moved off-screen. I could hear him scream, probably through a cushion, then he sat back down in front of us.

"How bad is it?" Gerald asked almost appearing serene.

Ford stood up, "Well Trixie here ordered ten and the supply request I received was for fifty."

Gerald's eyes went wide. "SO FORTY ARE MISSING?"

"Oh no, no no nooo," said Sue. "It's much worse than that. By my count we are down at least two hundred."

"TWO HUNDRED?"

"At least two hundred. But given the limited time, I have had to investigate so far… probably a lot more."

Gerald started crying, then he slammed his face into his desk a few times, before suddenly seeming to compose himself and then returned to looking at the camera calmly.

"The three of you probably deserve an explanation of why the Bureau Of Odd Biology is such a disaster," said Gerald. "I remember seeing all three of your photos slide across my desk as the people that Mr. Richard Head… Dick as you call him, had leaked information to about our founding project. Honestly, even if you hadn't I might have just informed you anyway. But well, you know how stupid it sounds to take horses, cows, and pigs, transform them into humans, and then dump them in minimum wage jobs?"

"Yes," I said in unison with Sue and Ford.

"Well. There was a senator named Philip Head. Yes, he is related to Dick, Philip is Dicks uncle. Anyway Senator Head was the numbskull who originally came up with that idea… and to make things worse he was the sort of visionary who didn't listen to other people telling him that something was a dumb idea.

"So Senator Head's project went ahead… ohh that rhymes… and to make sure no one criticized it, he made it secret. Naturally, and as a shock to everyone, the whole plan turned out to be a bad idea. And it was a little too embarrassing for the government to talk about so the whole thing was swept under the rug. The second batch was used on children so they were sent off to adoption centers… Hi Trixie, by the way I hope that worked out… and the first batch which were transformed as adults, well they didn't really know how to take care of themselves and… any that were still alive were cared for by the Bureau until they passed away naturally. Luckily someone figured out that information might leak and insisted upon that answer, given how loose Dick's lips are, a good bit of foresight. Anyway, most of the adults only lasted a few years… Senator Head put his nephew in the Bureau Of Odd Biology when it started, and insisted it remain open to protect his nephew. Also if the Bureau went defunct, the files might have been declassified, and this would look very bad in a re-election campaign so might as well kill two birds with one stone I guess. So Senator Head made the Bureau Of Odd Biology into the perfect place to dump your worthless son, daughter, niece, or nephew and hope that no one looked too closely.

"Richard for his part… seems determined to prove himself and to prove that the agency is useful to someone. So he started investigating cryptids, decided Bigfoot was real, set about proving it… and much like his uncle, refuses to let little things like proper procedure, reality or common sense get in the way. Probably in part because he gets all his knowledge on how to investigate from crime shows and thinks that gut instinct is equal to evidence."

Sue nodded and scratched her chin, "And aside from Dick, there are a whole lot of nepotism babies who might also want to prove themselves or think themselves protected from the law. Could one of those people steal some of the bug weed plants, and fake paperwork so no one notices?"

Gerald nodded, "Probably, this could be a problem, bug weed is basically the entirety of our actual jurisdiction, and the only useful thing we do. If there was an investigation because of this… all the people working here except the janitors and secretaries are someone's useless friend or relative. Senator Head is no longer a senator, but he still has friends in high places and might be mad if Richard was fired. If it was someone else… same difference, just another angry politician or high-level corporate executive."

"But we still need to pursue this," said Sue.

"I am begging you not to do that Ma'am," said Gerald. "Please… if you pursue, it will become an unholy mess. Seriously if you want to double-check that no one else is messing this up please do… but if you determine that it really is us… I would be happy to settle out of court."

"No," said Ford, "As I understand it, in the right hands, bug weed is the gateway of a medical revolution on the scale of vaccines, antibiotics, and anesthetics. In the wrong hands, well apparently there is at least one group of people turning people into sheep. I am concerned that this could be a serious issue. For that reason, we have to find out why."

Sue nodded, "That and when this goes to court it will be an absolute goldmine for us. People will freak out and all sorts of chaos will happen. And relatives of high-level politicians and corporate officers." She shook her head, "We can't just settle; nothing you could authorize would be worth it for us."

"Damn," said Gerald, "I guess I will see you in court… I hope there aren't any hard feelings on your end, but… if you really want to do this … my higher-ups will be very… intent on any mistakes you make. Even the slightest misstep and they will come down on you like a ton of bricks."

"We will be careful," said Sue, "I don't make mistakes, not when I am careful."

Gerald nodded, "For the sake of politeness, good luck." He then ended the call on his end.

Sue turned towards Ford and me. "I will get started with a subpoena," said Sue. "If we are lucky, Gerald's higher-ups will cave the moment there isn't any mistake for them to exploit."

"But if they don't, then this could take years," said Ford.

"We can apply the hurt to them and work on where the weeds are going," said Sue. "I can do two things at once. But with the right judge, we could probably walk all over them."

I nodded and got up to leave as this was my last thing for the day.

"Hold on," said Sue. "I just got a text message from an unknown number. It says to speak with Judge Jack Goaff."

I looked to Ford. He shrugged, "I never heard of the guy."

CHAPTER 12

It was a few days before we had another meeting. In the meantime, I helped Ford review the camera traps. We did not find anything out of the ordinary. Just ordinary animals, occasional weed bugs, and hikers and park rangers who left the plants alone. It looked as if nothing happened save for the one plant from the wild going missing. Ford reviewed the logs and no other plants were missing. Not from storage, locations in the wild, or any lab. The only place they seemed to disappear was in transit. Transit to the Bureau Of Odd Biology was full. Transit out from the Bureau Of Odd Biology was often missing eighty percent of the load.

Then we had another meeting and Sue brought us to Judge Jack Goaff.

Judge Goaff's office looked exactly like what you would expect the office of a judge to look like. Opulent, bookshelves lined with thick books, fine carpets, deep red curtains on the windows, and a big opulent, possibly mahogany, desk in the center.

Judge Goaff sat in his desk and looked like a stern teacher. He was showing his age, wrinkled face grey hairs, but still looked intimidating, in a 'maybe you can beat me in a physical fight but I will tear you apart verbally to the point that you will have wished to receive the pummeling' sort of way.

He gestured for us to sit in three chairs.

"I received your email Ms. Sue… and I am curious to what evidence you have that the Bureau Of Odd Biology had taken part in criminal activity."

"Well, for one your honor, every other piece of paper work checks out. We have proof that the ordered samples were collected by Ford and his fellow rangers, we have paperwork that Trixie and scientists like her received their orders. The number of samples requested and received by the scientists match. The samples requested from and sent by the rangers match. We have the paperwork and photographs to prove each step matches, except for the fact that Trixie made a request for ten and received that, and Ford received a request for fifty and sent it out."

Goaff nodded, "And the Bureau Of Odd Biology acted as middlemen, they were responsible for filtering and accepting orders. They could have easily modified the paperwork and taken the samples."

Sue nodded, "They were responsible for approving the orders and transferring the packages your honor. The envelopes are meant to be tamper-proof but they could have easily opened it, moved the contents, and faked the paperwork."

"That they could have, does not mean they did," said Goaff. "That someone did is not in debate… That the Bureau did specifically is… though I admit the evidence you have shown me so far is compelling. Tell me do you have something more, or is this all I have to think about."

Sue handed Goaff a small folder. "As it turns out, both Ford and Trixie took pictures of the package respectively before it was sent and after it arrived. As you can see…"

"These are different packages," said Goaff, alarmed. "Different signatures… the date stamp is visibly different ink;

the address is two lines on the first package but three on the second."

"You see the problem," said Sue.

Thus Sue and Goaff spent the next three hours speaking in legalese. I would say that most of their conversation went over my head, but most is a very weird way to say all.

Sue took Ford and me to lunch afterward and was smiling the whole time so apparently it went well. We went to Tiajuana Roadhouse: sombreros and Mexican-themed murals on the wall, corn chips with salsa, guacamole, and queso, the whole deal. I decided to try the false vegan tacos.

"Ok I have seen this several times and have to ask, what do they mean by false vegan tacos?" asked Sue.

"Plant meat," I said between bites. "Meat crops… gene modified crops that grow, say, a chicken breast instead of corn cobs. Some vegans and vegetarians think it is cheating but not all. Hence false vegan designation."

"Is that a legal definition?" asked Sue.

I nodded.

"As far as I know there have already been lawsuits of false vegan steaks tuning out to be real honest-to-goodness dead cow," said Ford.

"Interesting," said Sue. "I will have to look into this."

Within a week we had the warrant and Ford had gotten help from other rangers nearby along with the police.

We traveled to the Bureau Of Odd Biology head office, the building's label had all of the letters except the first letter of each word so small that you might miss them if you went looking. Thus B.O.O.B.

Ford handed the warrant to the secretary at the front desk who called down Mann.

"Some people are here. They say they have a warrant to search the building."

"On my way," said Mann.

A few minutes later, Mann arrived with another man in a suit. Ford handed the warrant to Mann who handed it to the man in a suit, who looked at it for a minute.

"Well you have all the paperwork in order," said the man in the suit. "Shame that I don't care." He then ripped the warrant in half, then the halves into quarters, then eighths, then sixteenths.

Ford chucked, "We made copies." He then produced one. Sue also brought out a copy of the warrant, so did I, and the twelve officers who were with us.

"F***," said the man in the suit.

"We aren't going to give you another one to rip up," said Sue. "So now you basically have to trust us as to what it… said."

The man in the suit looked down and sighed. "I should probably re-assemble that, and… prepare for trial."

"Based on what you just did, I would contact a lawyer."

"I am a lawyer."

"Then contact a better lawyer, who wouldn't rip up a warrant."

The suit-man/ bad-lawyer looked down, and started picking up the pieces of warrant.

Meanwhile, we got around to snooping. Obviously we couldn't get top secret documents, but anything else we could pick up and take home with us.

Looking around I found a lab… in an office… a large office but an office. I decided to call Sue over.

"Hey Sue," I shouted.

She arrived a moment later.

"This has some lab equipment... not all for biology, but some of what we would need to process bug weed."

"Interesting," said Sue; she turned to one of the officers.

"We will have to take some of these to examine in greater detail," said the officer.

Sue nodded, "Keep an eye out."

Ford walked up, "Whose office is this?"

Mann approached. "This office is used by Tio Samuel. He is... almost competent... some of the time. Often checks lab materials... you don't think he is a part of this do you?"

Sue shrugged, "It could be him or it could be someone borrowing the equipment."

Mann nodded, "I will get in touch with our lawyers."

Sue nodded, "Good."

Ford approached, "Um, should we really be telling them to have lawyers?"

Sue nodded, "My friends from law school need cases too. Plus, this way they won't be able to overturn a conviction for having bad legal counsel."

Ford grunted and nodded.

"If it makes you feel better, Mann had already made the decision to get a lawyer, nothing I say or do can change his mind. Also, to leave my comfort zone of scum-sucking lawyer, and start being an idealist." Sue shuddered, "I respect Mann for defending his employees, you don't see that all the time. I also trust the process, it is slow, imperfect on its best days, and frequently makes all sorts of mistakes, but it's the best tool we have to double-check ourselves. Even if Samuel is guilty, it is good that someone defended him, even if it's obvious, and that he worked solely out of malice, and that he would do it again. He deserves a fair trial. If you disagree, I look forward to prosecuting you when we all think that you are obviously guilty, obviously did it out of malice and are unrepentant, and have no one to defend you."

Ford stood there for a moment then nodded, "Do you really believe that?"

Sue shrugged, "It's what I say to people who don't like lawyers. It convinces them to let me do my well-paying job. Whether I believe a word of it or not is completely irrelevant. At the end of the day I like money, and I get paid a lot. I am also friends with a lot of lawyers, some of whom I regularly argue against. They like money too, and I want to keep in their good graces so when we meet up it is nice and civil and the judge doesn't get mad. And at the end of the day, I think this is how it should be. I have an incentive to do well, even if my heart is not in it. But I think a part of me does believe it. I might have to defend scumbags or prosecute saints, otherwise, no one would defend someone painted as a scumbag or prosecute a presumed saint."

Then I heard a kerfuffle.

We walked over to check it out and found two officers holding Dick to the ground.

"He tried to tackle me," said one of the officers holding him down.

"No they are lying," shouted Dick. "They just punched me." His face was bloody and a few bruises were forming.

"Stop lying," said the cop who then picked up Dick and dragged him out of the office.

I decided to snoop around Dick's office. I found lots of papers on Bigfoot, a poorly written article about the moon landing being fake. And a bag full of bug weed.

"Nice job with finding evidence," said Sue. "Unfortunately we got a problem."

"What problem?" I asked.

"The officer who arrested Dick turned off his body cam before that," said Sue. "Dick's lawyer is already preparing a defense based on that. In the end it shouldn't matter because the evidence is evidence, but it does make our position look worse. Police brutality and all, he might actually be honest this time."

CHAPTER 13

I had a day off so I did what I initially came here for. Measuring plants… I would say that I am starting to regret this whole thing, but I was already regretting it a long time ago. I got done late so the sun was down. To be fair it was winter, or nearly winter, so that was normal enough. Also, it was late enough that it probably would have been dark out anyway.

I got outside into the unlit parking lot. It was cloudy so there was no moon to light up my way; it wasn't snowing at the moment, but it had been earlier in the day. A shake of my cellphone activated its flashlight and then I could see enough to get to Hank and go back to the apartment. It was at this moment that I heard a kerfuffle to my left, far away from the street near the dumpster. With my cell phone flashlight, I got a glimpse of someone running away from the dumpster.

"Hello?" I shouted, in the general direction of the dumpster. I walked out into the parking lot. I kept the flashlight pointed at that area for a moment. Then I thought about the situation… I was a young woman, in the dark, in the middle of nowhere. Traffic was light enough that there was no one nearby, save for whoever was near the dumpster, and any cars that couldn't hear much outside of them anyway. In short, no one would hear me scream for help if I was attacked, and I was making a mistake on the levels of horror movie side character who dies to get the plot rolling.

I decided that discretion was the better part of valor and ran, well slid on the slush, to Hank. Once I was in, I turned him on and flipped on the headlights and carefully headed home.

Coming in the next morning Ford and Sue were having a conversation.

"So we have nothing?" asked Ford.

"Not nothing, just very bad for our cases, I recommend that we consider other options," said Sue.

"Are you sure? I mean given all that has happened."

Sue shook her head, "We can try but I am very doubtful of any result."

"Well… oh hello Trixie," said Ford to me. "We were discussing the case; it's not looking good."

"Given the evidence and an explanation from the lawyers of Dick and Tio, it's looking doubtful we could convince a jury," said Sue. "We may have to start over. Unless you have an idea."

"I think someone might have been going through our trash last night," I said.

Sue and Ford looked at me to explain, "I was leaving late and heard something."

"Someone went through our trash," said Ford "Is that Illegal?"

"Trixie thinks someone went through your trash," said Sue. "And no. Once it's in the garbage it's perfectly legal. At the same time, it is also not illegal to film someone going through your trash."

Fords eyes lit up, "Give me a second." He ran off, he returned a moment later with a camera in a box. I think it might have been a motion-activated camera. "We use these all the time, both to keep track of wildlife and also to monitor bug weed plants. If we set it up… where did you see this guy Trixie?"

"By the dumpster," I said.

"Right," said Ford, "By the dumpster… or in the dumpster, we might get a face."

"A face doing something perfectly legal," said Sue.

"True," said Ford, "But it might give us a lead onto something that is illegal."

"Do you put bug weed plants there?" I asked.

Ford looked at me and blinked, "No of course not." He went on, "Given their nature and how they are often used as a lab material or potential biohazard we burn any samples we don't use or send out."

"Then what will we find?" I asked.

Ford thought for a moment, "I don't know, maybe some documents not sensitive enough to be shredded before being tossed? I think that includes…"

"Includes what?"

"Known locations of bug weed plants," said Ford. "It was assumed it didn't matter because almost all of them are visible to the naked eye. Except in winter when the flowers die… we have found a few missing over winter… we thought it was animal life."

"Hold on," I said. "What about the specimens that failed to ship?"

Sue and Ford looked at me.

"She has a point," said Ford.

Sue stood there… maybe there is something we're missing. Anyway let's set up the camera and see. So I helped Ford set the camera up, and finished the actual work I came here for. At this point plan A was to enjoy the mountain during winter before heading home. But now I was still working on this never-ending investigation. I spent it doing the incredibly dull task of looking through old paperwork. My task was to find something that might be useful to someone trying to steal bug weed. The only thing was the differences in the shipping manifests. Fifty were requested, and ten were delivered, and stuff like that.

The next day, and my last full day here before I have to drive home we saw the recording. Ford, Sue, and I crowded around a laptop and saw the recording begin. The camera started rolling, and we all saw everyone's favorite person, Dick from B.O.O.B..

The man, still sporting a bruise from the rough arrest, stood in front of the dumpster, looked around, threw something in, something which looked like a piece of paper in a plastic bag, and then left. Ford grabbed latex gloves, and we ran outside through the snow to the dumpster.

"What is it?" asked Sue.

"It's a… poorly spelled, obviously fake, manifest for bug weed to be shipped from here directly to *Leaf It To Me*," said Ford, moving to show Sue the paper.

"So he is trying to frame us?" I asked.

"Yes," said Sue. "And if not, guess what… throwing stuff away in someone else's trash can is illegal."

"Wait, so going through someone else's garbage and taking whatever you want is fine, but the moment you add something new to it you're breaking the law?" I asked.

Sue nodded.

"That seems like an odd decision," I said.

"Yes," said Sue. "But that's not for us to decide, that's for the stupid, old, rich, white men, who we get tricked into electing every few years to decide."

"But we can arrest him for this?" said Ford.

Sue nodded, "I will get the paperwork started, we should be able to arrest him this afternoon… I have been looking forward to this for a long time."

Sure enough, that afternoon we had Dick, from B.O.O.B., in custody.

Ford came out of the interrogation room, and he simply shook his head. "He insists on speaking to a lawyer first."

"When does the lawyer get here?" I asked.

"We don't know. The guy he had walked out," said Sue.

"Maybe we should ask Gerald Mann to speed up the process," I said.

Ford shrugged, "If you want to, we still have his number."

So I called Mann on my cell phone.

"Hello, Trixie, Gerald Mann speaking, I saw your caller ID."

"Hey, can you get Mr. Head a lawyer, so we can speed up this process," I said. "He won't talk without a lawyer."

"I know," said Mann. "And yet, he is for now, not my problem."

"If we get him convicted he might not be your problem ever again."

"Ok, good point," said Mann. He then let out an exasperated sigh.

"Part of the problem," he began, "Is that he has required a lawyer so many times, and been quite rude to them, so that now most just refuse to take him as a client."

"What about the free lawyer a court will provide if you need one?" I asked.

Mann shook his head, "Richard always complains about how they are too busy and not motivated." Mann sighed, "To be fair he does have a point here… but it sucks all the same."

"So what are we supposed to do… get a lawyer for him?"

"You can try," said Mann. "But it seems like Ford and Sue are trying to find one, good luck."

So I returned empty-handed.

"No one wants to represent him," said Ford.

"Could we get someone who hates him to represent him? Just so that someone will," I asked.

"No," said Sue. "If you get a bad lawyer, that can be a good legal argument… desperate times call for desperate measures."

She then picked up the phone and called someone. "Hey Bruce… OK, you got me, I need a favor… sure if you can do this for me we can call it even for dealing with your Ex… have you heard of Dick from B.O.O.B.… yeah I need someone to represent him… because he is refusing to talk without a lawyer and I am connected to an investigation involving him… well it doesn't have to be you just a lawyer… you'll do it?… Thank you so much." She laughed, "Yes of course you can charge him, just as long as you represent him… Marks Jewels' police station… yeah I figured you could do this today… Thanks again bye."

She hung up and turned to us. "Bruce is an old lawyer preparing for retirement." She said, "He owes me a favor for helping him with his divorce, so he will help us by representing Dick."

"Is this wise" said Ford.

Sue shrugged, "Maybe not, I was hoping to hold onto this for a chance to embarrass him at his upcoming retirement party… but I have many ways to embarrass him."

"But… shouldn't someone else get him a lawyer?" asked Ford.

"We can get him one," said Sue. "And Bruce is good."

"So we are facing a good lawyer," I asked.

"If we win, we won't need to worry about Dick saying he was not well represented," said Sue.

"And if we lose?" I asked.

"That is always a risk," said Sue. "But if our case and evidence is good, and we have made no mistake, we should come out on top."

Ford nodded and turned to me "Trixie, could you go over some of the paperwork we got from B.O.O.B.."

I wrinkled my brow, "I thought you had already gone over them."

Ford began to sweat, "I did… but I would like someone to double check… just in case."

"You… didn't actually go over them, did you?"

Ford scratched the back of his head, looked up, seemed nervous. "Well… I was busy… and I don't have time to go over it today and… Sue might need something today… so."

Sue had her hands on her hips, looked at Ford, and in a voice that reminded me of an angry school teacher asked "Seriously?"

"Look, there was a thing with someone trying to smuggle ferrets, this was supposed to be a chill time of year… no pun intended… I'm sorry." Ford looked down for a moment, then he looked to me, "Trixie, can you help me, I have a phone call with the governor I have to make this afternoon and… can you do this for me?"

"I don't know," I said, "I was thinking about packing."

Sue perked up, "Offer her money."

Ford looked at Sue, then me, then shrugged, "Fifty dollars?"

Sue snorted, Ford turned to her, "What?"

"Just fifty for bailing you out? Back when I was in high school I used to put out for nerds who helped me with my homework." She smiled, "And I knew the material as well as they did."

Ford turned around gobsmacked.

"What, are you going to offer that?" said Sue with a coy look.

I decided to take a step back.

"NO," said Ford, "For one, that is probably illegal in multiple ways."

"I assure you… it is illegal in multiple ways," said Sue.

"And for another, my husband would be very angry with me if I did that," said Ford.

"Then let's see the stacks of cash," said Sue. "Trixie has bills to pay."

"The pile of papers isn't that thick," said Ford.

Sue raised an eyebrow.

"Ok, maybe it's half an inch thick." Ford turned to me, "Four hundred."

I looked to Sue, "Is it really half an inch thick?"

Sue nodded, "I recommend skimming."

"Ok," I said, "For four hundred."

"I recommend half now and half when she is finished," said Sue.

I nodded.

"Ok," said Ford, handing me the, indeed half an inch, thick folder. "Let me visit an ATM quickly."

He came back and handed me ten twenties, and I found a quiet place to put on some music and get to work.

After skimming for a while, I noticed a familiar address, the address of Calamites lab, and the order was the one I sent. I decided to see what happened in this mess and after an hour and too many paper cuts, I had the series of events complete. I went back to Sue and Ford with my findings.

"Any luck?" asked Sue.

"Yes actually," I said, "This is the order I sent in."

I handed Sue the first piece of paper.

"For ten plants," said Sue.

"This is it, as it reached Mr. Tio Samuel." I handed Sue another paper.

"Another ten," said Sue.

"This is it as it left Samuel's desk," I said, handing the third piece of paper.

"… For fifty," said Sue.

"And this is what logistics received," handing Sue five papers.

"One for you and four more to other addresses… where are these places…" Sue turned to Ford. "Ford would you care to actually do some minimal work and look up these addresses."

Ford sighed, "Sorry, I was busy, hold on." And he disappeared into the office and came back with his brick of a laptop.

After five minutes of typing Ford looked at Sue, "These four addresses… they are random houses."

"B.O.O.B. shouldn't be sending these materials out to random houses," said Sue. "Part of the regulations is that they are only supposed to be sent to licensed labs. Can I borrow your laptop?"

Ford handed Sue the laptop and she spent the next half an hour typing and clicking.

"Well, well, well," she said finally. "I have traced the owner of these houses through public records to M.S Robbin Banks." She turned to Ford, "I need to print out a few things."

"Go ahead, it's connected to the copier," said Ford.

A minute later Sue disappeared and returned with a small stack of paper. "Now I need to have a conversation with Dick, Bruce, Tio and Tio's lawyer. You two should go home and get some rest. Oh and Ford you owe Trixie and I two hundred dollars."

Ford sighed and opened up his wallet "Why did I take that bet?"

Sue giggled, Ford handed her, then me, two one-hundred-dollar bills. Then Sue dug out about sixty dollars from her wallet.

"Consider this a bonus for good work," she said.

I spend the rest of the day packing. In the morning I got a text from Sue.

"So it looks like Tio wanted to help out. He claims to have genuinely believed that Robbin was a researcher. He wanted to get someone to do more research on the plants. Apparently, he was not unaware of what bug weed transformations could do, and knew people who could have benefited from better cancer treatments, of cleaner and more full sex reassignment transitions. He meant well but got duped, at least according to Tio and his lawyer. Thus far no evidence disputes this claim, so we are tentatively pursuing a reduced sentence if he cooperates in helping us track down Robbin. He will probably get parole, assuming he can convince a judge that he was just dumb, not malicious. Bruce has taken up his case so he has a good chance of this mostly working out.

"Dick, as it turns out, was completely un-involved in these shenanigans, he just saw a coworker being arrested and he took action without thinking. Based on a conversation I had with Mann this is a completely normal thing for Dick to do.

"The juicy part of this is that B.O.O.B. should have done a better job of making sure that nothing like this was happening internally. Mann's argument is that his hands were tied by the powers that be, and he has shown… many emails, some text messages, and letters that support that claim. I am going to start the process of suing B.O.O.B. and Bruce might join me once he is done defending Dick and Tio

"I am not going to say that I couldn't have done it without you, but I am going to say that you were a massive help. The next phase is that we're are going to try and get Tio to send some samples out to Robbin, catch her, and then use that to track down the lab that actually produced the solution for *Leaf It To Me.*

"For now drive safely, I will be here for a few weeks, if you need me for anything, well you have my number."

CHAPTER 14

After the whole mess in Marks Jewels, I went back to Dedlam quickly. I spent a night in the apartment which felt almost abandoned. I promptly abandoned it the next day as mom and dad came down to pick me up for our annual Christmas trip. We visited my grandparents on my mom's side this year. We did all the usual stuff, exchanged presents, played games as a family, and watched a dozen different movies on the true meaning of Christmas. Grandpa expressed gratitude that "everyone came for what may be my last Christmas." Don't worry too much, he has been saying since I was negative three years old. Besides based on how he and Grandma were moving, I expected it would be at least a decade before I received any sort of inheritance from them.

We stayed at grandma and grandpas for New-Years and I got back home a few days into January. My next order of business was apparently speaking to Sick about a plan. Sue sent her partner Quick, a greying heavy-set man with a beard that made him look more like Santa Claus than a lawyer, to observe. We met in a brightly lit office with way too many paintings.

"So Sue tells me that you were helpful at Marks Jewels." He blinked a few times then began muttering under his breath, "That is such a bad name for a town." He shook his head.

"Anyway, based on what she said you did we are thinking about asking for your help," said Sick.

Quick cleared his throat, "What precisely would Trixie get out of this?"

"Well, two things, one, the satisfying feeling of doing the right thing, and two, money."

"How much money?" said Quick.

"Is that all you think about?" asked Sick.

Quick sighed, "One, the satisfying feeling of doing the right thing won't pay my clients bills, and two, you're married to my partner Sue. Therefor you should know very well that money is all we lawyers think about… I'm thinking about money right now. My wife told me I think about money more than sex… she is right."

Sick chuckled, "Well I have bad news on that front, the pay scale is not great… most of our budget is spent on fancy equipment, not anything more effective like hiring people who can use that equipment effectively. But it would look good on a resume, assuming other police officers don't screw that up, but it might work for a bit."

"How legal would it be?" I asked.

"You should let me ask these questions," said Quick, "But yes."

"We can get her trained up over the spring," said Sick. "Have her come in over the weekend. She does her classes and learns what we need in her off time. The fact that she was able to find a very important aspect of the case in Marks Jewels might help us."

"She will need assurances of legal protection… and if necessary, witness protection," said Quick.

Sick nodded, "We can do that."

"She will be risking her life, possibly the life of her family, for what exactly? A good feeling and how much money?"

"$500 a month during training and $2000 a month during the actual investigation over summer."

"How long?"

"Four months with an option to extend if necessary."

"Not looking good," said Quick.

Sick nodded, "I know she is not power-hungry, so I hope that she is driven to do the right thing."

"Cause this pay won't cut it otherwise," said Quick. He turned to me, "I would recommend you sleep on this, maybe reach out in a week or two, there is no rush."

I nodded, "I will let you know when I make a decision." I could feel my heart racing.

"I will be honest," said Sick, "It is a big ask, but I will do everything I can to protect you. You would be a police informant, and that gives us some leeway to help you, even if you have to break the law at some point. It will be hard, but I wouldn't ask you if I didn't think you were up to the challenge."

I nodded, "Give me some time to mull it over."

"Of course," said Sick.

CHAPTER 15

It took most of the following spring to get me ready to go undercover, and it felt cool to say it out loud. I had my degree in hand and this would work as a job for now. I was even getting paid OK for this gig, enough to make rent and feed myself… barely.

I took Hank down to *Sodom Hill,* it was somehow even more in the middle of nowhere than *Leaf It To Me.* Lots of wheat fields, and not much else, surround the area. It would be a seven-hour drive to Nowhere… literally, that was the name of the town. The drive actually took ten hours, due to a flat tire. But I made it to Nowhere and got to the one-bedroom apartment I was renting for the next few months.

I started the long process of getting my stuff inside from Hank, the poor guy was full of my junk. For tonight though, I was exhausted, so I just got a mattress, some bedding, and other basic supplies in, and fell asleep.

I woke up late the next day, it was fine. I had the whole day to move in, got showered, had breakfast, and noticed that I had three missed texts.

"Yo, Trixie, this is your new boss, Snow, but you will refer to me as Mr. Leatherfall. I own you now, and am very crazy so you had better not try anything like that last guy. I need you in today, I don't care if it's your day off, get your butt in here now."

Doesn't he sound pleasant? That was from three hours ago, 8:00 am, my starting time was 9:00, and also not for another two days. The next two were also from him.

"Trixie, you had better get your butt over here… we need you now if you're not in in five minutes your fired. I mean it… DON'T DUCK WITH ME?"

I think that he messed up and put a question mark where he meant to put an exclamation mark. I also doubt he meant "Duck" but probably some other word and that got hit by the auto-correct. I was also tempted to respond with "you're". That text was two hours ago. Though honestly, if I was fired before I arrived at this point, I might accept that.

"YOU ARE FIRED TRIXIE, but maybe if you arrive, I will let you beg for your job back."

At this point, I had just enough coffee to wonder if he might actually be bluffing. I decided to give him a call.

"AH TRIXIE." He shouted into the phone so loud I had to hold it away from my ear. "FINALLY, ANSWERING YOUR GOD DAMN PHONE, IS THIS JOB NOT IMPORTANT FOR YOU?!?!?!?"

"I just woke up because I was not scheduled to come in until Monday." I began, "And I had a long…."

"I DON'T CARE WHAT THE SCHEDULE SAYS, YOU WORK FOR ME, I OWN YOU, YOU COME IN WHEN I SAY, THAT MEANS ANY TIME OF ANY DAY. DO YOU GET ME?"

At this point, I was too tired to deal with the bull. "Really? I thought I was fired a couple of hours ago, if so, you don't own me anymore."

"I AM MERELY LETTING YOU BEG FOR YOUR JOB BACK, NOW GET YOUR BUTT IN HERE, I NEED YOU NOW."

"If you really need me, you can't fire me," I said.

"I CAN DO THE JOB MYSELF IF I HAVE TO, BUT IF I HAVE TO, I WILL FIRE YOU AND NOT LET YOU BEG FOR YOUR JOB."

"Right… I will be there in a bit."

"FIVE MINUTES OR YOU'RE FIRED… I mean uh, UNTIL I WON'T LET YOU BEG."

He then hung up, no doubt feeling very proud of himself.

I then changed out of my casual home clothes, and into my "Work Clothes" which was mostly old stuff as I doubted I would be in a suit and tie job based on the description. Though having just met Snow I was starting to wonder if the description might not match the job.

I got there fifteen minutes after the call. I wanted to look sad, to cry up a storm, but in my tired state, the best I could manage was to look only mildly mad.

Sodom Hill was run down, the paint was falling off the sides of the barn, the parking lot was paved though filled to the brim with cracks. Half of the wood fencing looked like it was about ready to fall to pieces, the other half looked like it had already fallen to pieces and been patched back up.

"HOW LONG DOES IT TAKE TO GET HERE?" shouted a voice that sounded exactly like Snow. He was worse dressed than I was and looked hideous, it looked like he almost shaved that morning, was balding, and smelled like he never showered but smoked every day. A cigarette tray in his office attested to one of those things.

"IF YOU CAME TO BEG YOU'RE OFF TO A BA…" at that point Snow's tirade was interrupted when he tripped and fell flat on his face. I think that might be part of why he is so ugly.

"Are you done tripping on yourself?" I asked, internally cursing myself for letting that slip… well the worst that might happen is I go home saying it didn't work out.

Snow got up, "I AM FINE!" he shouted with a bloody nose, "I AM TOUGHER THAN CONCRETE."

I rolled my eyes and decided to gamble this whole thing on being a stupid bluff. I turned around and started to walk away.

"WHERE ARE YOU GOING?" shouted Snow.

I turned around slowly, "You called me over here because you needed me, a new hire. Either whatever this is can wait, in which case stop wasting my time, or it can't, in which case firing me would mean you have to do it yourself."

"IT'S ALREADY DONE WHICH IF YOU WANT YOUR JOB BACK YOU CAN EAT MY BUTT."

I decided to walk away just in case he meant it literally.

"WHERE ARE YOU GOING?"

"Bu bye," I said.

"Whuu… WAIT," said Snow.

I stopped and turned to look at him, I could see the sweat on his face and he was shaking, for the first time he didn't look angry, he looked afraid.

"I will start on Monday, 9:00 am, not one minute before, we clear?"

"I… yes," said Snow, starting to relax, "I will see you Monday."

I then left the raggedy building and drove Hank, still full of my stuff, back to the apartment. And began my long day of moving in. The apartment block itself was made of small, two-story buildings with concrete walkway balconies for the second floor, up a flight of stairs, mine was at the far end of the second floor. There were no elevators and only one stair way.

I got two loads up and was getting the third in when I encountered someone from a single apartment in front of mine.

"Need help moving in?" asked a reasonably handsome blond guy maybe a year or two younger than me; he was wearing shorts and a t-shirt.

I wasn't sure it was a good idea to trust him… but he didn't look shady, the apartment parking lot was well-lit, and I was too tired to say no.

"Sure," I said, "give me a minute and I will give you something to carry."

I put that load down and walked down with my new neighbor to Hank to load that guy up.

"What is your name?" I asked when we got to Hank.

"Trip," he said.

I loaded him up with clothing

"I am Trixie, nice to meet you," I said, grabbing part of my bed frame.

"Likewise," said Trip. He then helped me get my stuff into my apartment. He even volunteered to help me assemble my bed frame.

"So what are you going to do here?" asked Trip. "Not very many people move to this place."

"I will be working at Sodom Hill," I said.

Trip froze, and looked down. "Good luck, they have… incredible turnover." He perked up "Listen there are other places in town, I got a job at *Like no Udder*, it's a restaurant, they do lots of stuff with cheese, I can put a good word in with the manager there… if Sodom Hill doesn't work out."

"You seem concerned," I said.

"I am… I used to work at Sodom Hill, only made it three months, and I stuck it out for two of them only because my dad was in charge."

"Is your father… Snow Leatherfall?" I asked with wide eyes.

"I take it you have had the displeasure of meeting him," said Trip. "But as much as I hate it… yes he is. *Like no Udder* has very good benefits for a restaurant… they are also closed Sunday and Monday, so you are guaranteed two days off… and also, they're closed for most holidays."

"Thanks for the advice," I said, "But… is it just Snow or is Sodom Hill bad for other reasons?"

Trip sighed and shook his head, "My father likes to bully people into coming in on their days off," said Trip. "By the way don't fall for it, he won't fire you for refusing to come in on your day off, he will just pretend he will. Every. Single. Day. Off. You. Will. Ever. Have."

"He doesn't stop when you refuse to take it seriously?" I asked.

Trip shook his head.

"How does he keep people?"

"He doesn't." Trip slumped onto the floor, "Most people who work for him last only a month or two before they quit, if they even make it that long. Some just seem to drop off the face of the Earth, he spends most of his day trying to hire people. Frankly, I'm shocked he can find any help at all."

"I see," I said wishing I had said no to going in as an informant.

"It's not just my father, the animals at his farm always try to hurt people. Or break out of their cages. I got bit by the most hostile lamb in existence, twice. The second one is what drove me to quit. The fences are terrible, you will spend most of your time trying to catch runaway sheep, they will get away, trust me, and then he will yell at you and act like he is going to fire you, but if you try to walk away, he will start bargaining… my father is a stupid man."

I just shook my head, "Well… I will let you know how long I make it," I said thinking about where I would go on vacation after this just to feel better. I think a cruise sounds nice.

"I hope you find something better soon, good luck," said Trip.

After he left I called Sick, "I have gotten moved in, good news, may have made friends with Mr. Leatherfall's son; bad news, I already want to quit."

"Ohhh no," said Sick, "I did say that the site was very badly reviewed by employees, didn't I?"

"Yeah, I may have found part of the reason why, if the son is correct, there are many more."

"Keep the recording device on during your first day of work, I might be able to get you a raise on our end."

"Thank you."

CHAPTER 16

So I got to work on Monday, arrived on time, 8:59 am. "WHAT SORT OF TIME DO YOU CALL THIS?" shouted Snow, who came marching over and tripped on the same patch of ground he tripped on yesterday. This time he had a cigarette in his mouth.

He got up again, "I AM FINE!!!!" he said with another bloody nose and a new minor burn on his face. "WHERE WERE YOU?????????"

"This is my starting time, if you like I can leave now," I said, already fed up.

"NO, DON'T, just ahhh, JUST GET TO WORK AND DO YOUR JOB."

"Where is that?" I asked, "What do you need?"

"OHHH. MOMMY I WANT HELP BECAUSE I AM STUPID AND..." it was at this point that he probably noticed I had turned around.

"WAIT, NO... with Justin, he will show you around, he is in that building," he said pointing to the shed behind me.

I went inside and ran into a plain faced dark-skinned man; his nametag said Justin Time.

"Hello, you are Trixie I presume?" said the man.

"Yeah, Justin?" I said, walking into the lab.

We shook hands.

"I will only be working with you today. I put my two weeks' notice in, exactly fourteen days ago. My mother is insisting I give doing what I love another chance and promised that she would help me find an actually good job. Says that she could see my soul being sucked out of me."

I chuckled, "You are doing a great job of selling this position," I said.

"You only think you are being sarcastic, in time you will see that I actually am," said Justin. "I will walk you through the normal stuff for today, for everything else, I leave you the book, it contains instructions on how to do everything I won't be showing you."

"Who else works here?" I asked.

Justin laughed for a solid minute then he looked me in the eye, "Oh… you were serious… that's even funnier!" and he then laughed for another minute.

"I don't even know why I am bothering with the name tags," he said after he stopped laughing. "We are the only two people here today… you are one of only two people I have ever worked with here directly… the other guy quit on my first day too… there are maybe a handful of other employees, but I doubt you will get to know them very well. Sometimes I feel lucky to have PPE, er, Personal Protective Equipment. Certainly Snow thinks he is the most generous boss ever to supply us with anything that we need. We should exchange emails… if I find a better job, I might try to recruit you into it."

I sighed, "Let's just get this day over with," I said.

Justin then spent all day showing me how things worked. He made a point to show me that the shower and eyewash stations were broken… and claimed that they had been that way when he got there and that his predecessor claimed the same thing. Just before we left at 6:00 he gave me one final piece of advice.

"Snow will almost always give you work at the end of the day. Like last minute. Fridays are very bad because he will wait until you are about ready to go home and demand a week's worth of work done today."

Like clockwork, Snow Came by. "HEY SHOVEL FACE AND NEW WHICH GET THESE SAMPLES DONE TODAY."

He then left before I could ask why he didn't give us this earlier.

"He also likes to give out busy work, if he sees you have nothing to do he will give you something to do, good luck ever getting out on time. Oh, and when he calls you on a day off, just don't answer, it's all bluff... learned that after one week."

"Got it," I said as I began to regret agreeing to do this.

"Also don't worry about over time, you won't be getting any because it's a 'salaried position.'"

I just shook my head.

So we got to work and I noticed that the recipe was very similar to the solution that turned me into a sheep the first time, as well as the solution to change back, but this one seemed to include plant matter at the part where DNA was extracted. No, I did not like the idea of that.

Ultimately, we left nearly five hours late. Justin told me that this was normal, I was motivated to find whatever dirty laundry Snow had just to get this over with.

Tuesday was worse as I was by myself and already tired, got back to the apartment at 11:30 pm. By Wednesday I was envious of retail workers, a position I never thought I would consider working at. When I got home Thursday I was wondering if I could somehow trade places with someone whose job involved being neck-deep in sewage all day. The best part of Friday was that I remembered to sneak out my phone to take a photo of the instructions. Oh, and that I got to sleep in all day Saturday.

In the early morning, I ignored my phone which had Snow trying to call me as long as I could, then I turned it off and went back to sleeping, got up around 11:00, and turned my phone back on, only for Snow to blow up my phone with texts again. Then I actually got one from Sick.

"Hey Trixie, first off thanks for the pic, good evidence, physical copy, if possible, would be great. Also, a sample of any odd organism would also be great. Lastly, we did a check on Trip, and he seems to be OK. See if you can interview him to set us up to talk. Thanks!"

I decided to do that later, see if I saw Trip around as I had to go shopping today… yay more work on my "day off."

After screaming in despair for what must have been five minutes, I heard a knock on the door. I checked the peephole and it was Trip, I went ahead and opened up.

"Oh my… you OK?" he asked, giving me a hint as to how bad I must look right now.

"I'm… no… not really," I said.

"I felt that way after working with my father too… sorry for bothering you, I just wanted to check up."

He turned away and I was going to just let him go… I needed to talk to him but didn't care. Then I heard Sue's voice.

"Hello, pardon me," said Sue to Trip, as she walked along the balcony, then she turned to me "Hey Trixie."

"Hello, Sue," I said.

"Your Mother?" asked Trip.

"No, I'm her lawyer."

"If you are here to sue my father, I can help you."

"Who is your father?"

"Snow Leatherfall."

"What a coincidence, you must be Trip."

"Um… Yes."

"Perfect, Trixie can we borrow your apartment for a moment?"

"Ummmm, sure," I said.

We sat inside the one-room apartment, I took the bed, Trip leaned against the wall next to the bed, and Sue took the center of the room.

"So the short version, we think that there is something very, very nasty happening at Sodom Hill," said Sue.

Trip blinked a few times, "You mean like mistreating employees?" asked Trip.

"Well, yes but also something else… something that may arguably be worse. Did anything change in your father, in the fall last year?"

"Yes," said Trip, "It was around then he started routinely making people stay late, having them work on busy work during normal hours, and everything else became overtime. It's part of what caused me to quit."

"Interesting… around that time, my husband raided another shady farm that had been doing work with human trafficking, a note leads us to here."

"Your husband?"

"She is married to a police officer," I said.

Trip nodded, "You don't think my father deals in human trafficking, do you?"

"We think it's possible," said Sue. "My husband's boss asked me to work with prosecution here. You said he changed… what was he like before?"

Trip shrugged, "At home, he was tolerable, quick to anger, but would calm down, talk about his farm project thing… though I don't think he mentioned people, it was always the sheep."

"Sheep." I asked, "What kind of sheep?"

"He called them Sapi sheep," said Trip. "Something about them being super smart sheep, was convinced they would be the next big thing in sheep."

Sue cocked her head, "As in petting zoo?"

Trip nodded, "That and also being more able to watch themselves than regular sheep. He was convinced they would make him rich. Then something went wrong, started blaming everyone for his problems. Me, mom, his friends, family, employees, random strangers, everyone."

Sue leaned forward, "It is possible that if he is connected to the other case, and if they were his first and only buyer…. That might explain the change."

Trip frowned at Sue, "Part of me wants to believe my father is better than this," Trip began to slide to the floor, "but he is a jerk on his best days. And he started getting more concerned about money."

"I see," said Sue.

"Unfortunately, I have recently moved out and am going no contact with my parents. If they try to talk to me again, I might actually let them talk to me and tell you anything."

Sue nodded, "I will give you my number in case you hear anything. If not, or if you can't face them don't worry about it."

"Um… how much will this cost? I don't have money."

"Oh, don't worry, my husband's work is paying me. The only person I will be sucking dry is him," she winked at us.

I then had time to go shopping and get my groceries. Sunday was thankfully calm as I only had to argue with Snow for a minute. Then came Monday, back to work.

Snow came out, storming in a rage, as usual, this time holding a large bottle of hand soap.

"WHAT IS THIS?" he asked.

"Um… soap… why."

"LOOK AT THIS," he said pointing to the words, "Vegan, cruelty-free" on the soap bottle.

"So?" I asked.

"IT'S VEGAN."

"Um… accurate."

"WHY?"

"Because vegans exist…"

"WHY DO WE HAVE IT?"

"Because we need to keep our hands clean."

"WHY DO WE HAVE VEGAN SOAP?"

"I don't know. I didn't buy it."

I was getting fed up at this point.

"BUT WE HAVE IT, I DON'T WANT THIS SISSY STUFF, IF MY HANDS ARE CLEAN, I WANT TO KNOW A COW DIED TO MAKE IT HAPPEN."

"But…why?"

"I DON'T WANT THIS FREAKING SISSY IDIOT VEGAN SOAP," said Snow, throwing the bottle onto the ground hard enough to break the plastic bottle with a horrible cracking sound. Soap spewed everywhere, mostly onto Snow. It was then that we both became aware that in between the soap and the ground was Snow's foot. His strained expression and a single tear falling down his face made it clear that part of the horrible cracking sound, was Snows foot.

"GO… get me a new bottle. Not this sissy vegan stuff," said Snow.

"Ok…" I said, "Will you reimburse me?"

"JUST… give me the receipt, leave it on my desk."

"Anything else while I am out… such as a bandage?"

"What… no of course not, just the soap, I'm fine."

I decided not to argue with Snow and went off to the local grocery store to find non-vegan soap. A less petty woman would have gotten something cheap in a large bottle, I was not that woman, I went with something expensive in a small bottle. After double-checking to make sure it said vegan nowhere on the bottle, I made the purchase and drove back. Snow was nowhere to be seen.

I went to put the receipt on his desk. I found a note handwritten in all caps.

"I WILL BE BACK TOMORROW, LEAVE THE RECIPT HERE AND GO HOME. DON'T TOUCH ANYTHING."

Obviously I did as instructed, once I had translated the misspelled word receipt. Only I ignored the part about going home and not touching anything. I took some quick photos of the desk and what was on it, not looking too deeply in case Snow might have noticed something was misplaced. Then I looked outside of the labs for the first time.

It was a farm, nowhere near as nice as *Leaf It To Me*, which is saying something. If there was any not-rotten wood, I was not able to find it. If there was metal, it was rusted. The Sapi Sheep were very angry, baa-ing at me loudly at all times.

"You guys OK?" I asked the sheep.

One responded by head-butting the fence with his horns.

"Don't stick your hand in," said a voice from behind me. "They bite."

"Um… hello?" I said turning to see the source of the voice, a middle-aged man in raggedy overalls carrying straw over his shoulder.

"You must be the new lab boy, even though you're a lady."

I nodded, "Yeah I am the lab person."

"Snow goes through you guys like frat boys go through plastic cups. Every few months I see a new one of youse in the lab, or wandering around looking for something. I think I caught you working in the lab once, but not much special there."

"Right," I said, "My predecessor trained me for one day before he left."

"So did the guy before him, and the guy before that quit in a huff one day, and the guy before her just disappeared off the face of the earth. I honestly don't know what he is doing to youse, but last year he went through twenty-four different people over the course of the year. I am not a manager but he is definitely doing something wrong with youse."

"Is he not just a terrible boss all around?" I asked when suddenly one of the sheep head-butted the metal pole I had been leaning on, startling me slightly.

"Don't worry about them, they are always angry. But I don't know," said the man, "He pays me alright, I'm here every day but only for a bit, just feed the sheep and go home. Only takes eight hours a day. Best job I ever had."

"You serious?" I asked.

"Yep," said the man, "I should introduce myself, my name Stuck, Stuck Holms."

"Um… Trixie Night," I said back. "Yes I know it sounds like the name of a pony, I had that name when my birth parents put me up for adoption. I might try to change my name one day."

Stuck chuckled, "Yeah… maybe after you inevitably quit, everyone else does, even the guys he gets to help me. Last one quit after two days."

"Yikes," I said thinking that I would have done the same if I could have.

"Yeah," said Stuck, "Still you probably have nothing to do today, Mr. Leatherfall fell and broke his foot, he called his wife to get him to the hospital. I assume that is why you are back here?"

"Yeah just looking around before I head home," I said.

Stuck nodded, "Just be careful around these guys, they are very aggressive and will bite and head-butt and stomp on you if you give them a chance. Don't know why."

I was, at this point, thinking that the why might be because they were once human, and remember that on some level, and are fighting us because they think we did this to them. Boy, am I glad that I didn't say it out loud. If it hadn't happened to me I would have thought that to be crazy.

Stuck moved on to do whatever. So I crouched near the sheep pen.

"You used to be a person, didn't you?" I whispered to the sheep.

One ram got very agitated and pushed the others out of its way to head-butt the fence.

"Hey, I am not going to hurt you," I said.

The ram then baaed at me, but it almost sounded like he was trying to say something.

"Baaave, buuu, buuuun."

I was not sure what the ram was trying to say, but I decided that now was as good a time as any to leave and head back to my abode.

The next day during my all-too-short lunch break I talked with Stuck.

"So how long until you bail?" he asked.

"Not sure," I said, "Some issues on my end."

"Hmm, you might still be here in a few months, maybe then you will find whatever you are actually looking for."

"Maybe."

"But like everyone else who has ever worked here one day you will be gone."

"Have you kept in touch with any of them? The former employees I mean?"

"Some, many told me that they didn't want any reminders of this time, or that they didn't want Leatherfall to have any way of contacting them through me. Some I have on Twitface, others just one day seemed to fall off the face of the Earth."

I didn't like that last idea. If you can turn people into sheep, and if someone goes missing, put two and two together… of course, I had no proof that Snow was doing that, he could, in theory, do it, but that doesn't mean he would, or did. Someone would have noticed something right? Still, when I had a moment, I texted Sick.

"Talking with another employee here, said that some people fell off the face of the earth? Any missing person reports connected to this place?"

After several hours of work, I got a few minutes to check my phone, Sick had responded.

"Looks like a yes, the last guy, Justin turned up elsewhere, but there are twenty missing person reports that were last employed at Sodom Hill. There is also a report about potential police corruption, I would be on high alert."

I did not sleep well that night.

CHAPTER 11

So I got back to the farm on Tuesday; Snow looked as unhappy as ever. So I got to the lab and started working. About five minutes in I heard Snow shouting at someone, then a girl came in with tears flowing down her face.

"Um… Hello," I said, "You OK?"

"Oh… yeah, fine, just, terrible first day," said the girl. "Um… I am apparently supposed to work with Trixie."

"That's me," I said, "You got a name?"

"Mary."

"Nice to meet you Mary."

"Likewise."

Mary was slightly shorter than me, blond, freckles on her face, green eyes, and based on what her tears had done, it looked like she wore makeup.

I showed her around the lab, and helped her get started. We kept going until lunch, we chatted some more then.

"So yeah, first day… not great," said Mary.

"Sorry," I said.

"It's not your fault," she said, "Is it?"

"Well, no… but I am still sympathetic."

"Was your first day here horrible?"

"Every day has been horrible."

"I see."

"Hopefully with two people the work will get done faster, but I have a feeling that it just means Snow will give us more."

Mary looked down at the floor for a moment, then she turned back to me, "Maybe we could apply elsewhere together?"

"I am stuck here for the time being," I said, "But who knows." I wasn't about to say that I had gotten involved with legal nonsense.

In an unsurprising twist, we finished late, and I was going to my good old car Hank when I saw something. It was Dick, from B.O.O.B.

He was looking less like law enforcement, and more like a creepy stalker hiding in the grass.

"OUT OF MY WAY," shouted Snow, marching somewhat into me, carrying something in a bunch of glass mason jars. A moment later I noticed he was marching directly towards Dick, from B.O.O.B., and that while Dick seemed to notice, Snow had not.

I could have said something to avert a clueless Snow tripping over Dick and falling all over him, I could have but I chose not to.

"What is Dick from B.O.O.B. doing here?" asked Mary. As the inevitable happened and Snow tripped over and fell onto Dick.

"You know him too?" I asked.

By this point, Dick and Snow had both gotten up and started glaring angrily at each other in the exact way that actually mature men don't.

"He was trying to investigate my Biology 104 class for making glowing Daphnia, got yelled at by a judge, and left us alone."

"Similar story," I said, "I was doing some work with my advisor and he came to harass her until a judge told him to back off."

By now these two grown men were shouting at each other in the way that actually mature men don't.

"Should we do something?" asked Mary.

"Get popcorn and watch?" I suggested, half-jokingly.

Mary tilted her head, "I've got pretzels in my car."

I nodded, "That will work."

Mary then trekked to her car and grabbed a bag of pretzels, and ran back, standing at my left. The bag was open but clipped shut, until she removed the clip and offered the open end of the bag to me.

I took out a handful as did Mary, and watched these two grown men have a tantrum.

Just as the first pretzel entered my mouth, Snow and Dick attempted to punch each other. I say attempted because they both missed each other's face, fell over toward each other bonked heads, and fell on the ground.

"Is that it?" asked Mary with what you could call a hint of disappointment, if you could say that habanero peppers had a hint of spiciness, but then the two combatants stood back up. They glared at each other and tried to punch each other again. This time Snow got Dick in the face, while Dick aimed below the belt. When Snow doubled over, Dick got him in the face knocking Snow to the ground.

"I think it is time to call it in," I said to Mary as Dick lifted up his leg to stomp on Snow's face. Though before I could make the call, Snow got a kick in on the leg Dick was standing on, knocking him down.

"We can continue to watch till the popo show up," said Mary, as both men got back up onto their feet.

I downed a final pretzel as the two men flailed ineffectively at each other, and called 911 on my phone.

"911, what is your emergency?" said the tired-sounding man on the other end of the line.

"My boss is fighting a government official person," I said as the two men stopped flailing and Dick tried and failed to land another below-the-belt hit.

"Ok, dispatching an officer… wait… is the government official… Mr. Richard Head from the Bureau Of Odd Biology?"

"Yes," I said.

"And… no, no, no, is your location… is your boss, Mr. Snow Leatherfall?"

"That is the one." By this point, the two men had gotten each other good in the face a few times and were bleeding rather badly.

"I am sending an officer, and a couple of ambulances, stay out of the fight. Are you safe? What the heck am I asking, those two are so pigheadedly stubborn that once they start fighting they won't notice you're there."

"We are safe for now." Just as I said that the two men head-butted each other and both fell over unconscious. "Update, I think they knocked each other out."

"Ok… Don't get too close as they may still be violent. Can you tell from where you are standing if they might still be alive?"

I squinted to see, but I think I saw their chests moving up and down.

"I think they are still alive," I said into the phone.

"Damn," said the dispatcher under his breath "Ok… Police and medical care should arrive soon, hopefully before they wake up."

Then Snow got up and started to shuffle towards Dick, Dick rolled, and pushed himself up to a sitting, and then a standing position. The two men glared at each other, clenched their fists, threw punches, missed, and then fell into each other and back onto the ground.

"They just got up for a bit, but fell back down," I said to the phone.

"Honestly I know this is going to sound horrible," said the 911 operator. "But those two have been a thorn in many people's side for a long time, the only reason I am not snacking on something while listening to you is because I can't eat at the desk."

"My co-worker and I have pretzels."

"Ohh, have one for me."

I did so, and Mary and I snacked until the police and ambulance showed up. A very angry-looking, bald African American man in a police officer uniform got out of the car and marched over to Snow and Dick.

He looked down at the two of them, snorted as if in disgust, while Snow and Dick tried to crawl away... very slowly. The officer then approached us while two more went to place handcuffs on Snow and Dick and the EMTs followed them.

The officer approached us and glanced at us quickly.

"You two OK?" he asked.

"I'm fine," I said.

"Me too," said Mary.

"You sure that neither of these two *cough cough* gentlemen so much as bled on you today?"

I looked at Mary who shook her head. "No why?" I asked.

"Because I want to see these two rot in jail after all the trouble they caused... but both have their God Damn connections." He looked down towards a camera on his chest. "I don't think I am a bad cop; I was willing to have these body cams implemented on my uniform, in fact, I argued for them after a cousin got hurt in a raid gone wrong. But today, just today… you two get out of here, I will want to speak with you sometime tomorrow if you have time."

"Um, should I bring a lawyer?" asked Mary.

"It can't hurt," said the cop, "If only to stop their lawyers from claiming you said something stupid."

"I can hook you up," I said to Mary. "I have a lawyer friend in town anyway."

"Hope she is not too expensive," said Mary.

"If she is, ask for a public defender," said the officer. "Let's get some contact information from you two and see if we can arrange a meet-up. Names Lou by the way."

The next morning, I got an angry text from Snow.

"HA HA I GOT OUT OF JAIL EVEN THOUGH YOU CALLED THE POLICE ON ME, GET BACK TO WORK I OWN YOU."

I called Lou.

"Yeah," he said gritting his teeth. "Apparently his cousin is the sheriff, and that family looks out for each other. The other guy, Dick, he had some connections as well and got out. I did get to talk to your lawyer friend though and I think we can make both of these jerks hurt."

"For now, I would just go to work as normal. Or quit, your call. Keep in touch. And we will work this out."

I got to work a little late and ignored Snow's shouting, and took some solace in him falling down on his face again.

I didn't see Mary that day, I had her number and texted her asking if she had quit. No response. I tried calling her over my lunch break, no response.

Things were quiet for a bit so I took a break and walked around the sheep paddock, one sheep, in particular, seemed to Baaa-ing at me and stood itself up on the fence. It seemed less aggressive than the others, so I gave it a pat. It seemed distressed as I went back.

I called Mary again, and as I was walking, I heard a phone go off, in a trash can. I canceled the call and the phone stopped ringing. I sent a text to Mary, the phone in the trash can went off, I called again, and the phone rang. Mary is missing… something happened to her… these are Sapi sheep…

"Oh God, please, no," I said to myself as I ran back to the sheep.

"Um… OK this is baaad," I said to the herd of sheep, and they got quiet and stared at me.

I looked around. The coast looked clear.

"Is… Mary here?"

One sheep, I think it was the same friendly one, started baaing like crazy and running in circles.

"Ok, to prove it… stomp three times if Dick and Snow fought last night."

The sheep stomped 3 times.

"Ok… now two times if they used Tasers and three if they used knives." The sheep tilted her head.

"Ok, that was a trick question. One more, about how many hours did you work yesterday, stamp the ground once per hour."

The sheep, Mary, responded with 13 stamps.

"Ok, I believe you now Mary." She bahh-ed.

"Everyone else, I will try to help you… but I need Mary first… I will come back for the rest of you."

The sheep made a hole for Mary who ran up to the fence, I lifted her out and placed her on the ground next to me.

"I will come back for the rest of you, promise," I said to the sheep. "Let's go to my car," I said to Mary we then ran to the front of the building. I unlocked Hank and opened the driver-side rear door. Mary hopped into the back, and I closed her in before moving to the driver's seat.

"WHAT ARE YOU DOING?" shouted Snow.

I got into the driver's seat and closed the door, hitting the lock all button.

"GET BACK HERE," shouted Snow, running much quicker than I thought he could. "GIVE ME MY SHEEP BACK."

I turned Hank on… "Please don't fail me now," I said to Hank as the engine cranked. By this time Snow was at my door grabbing the handle.

"UNLOCK THIS CAR YOU WITCH," shouted Snow, before Hanks's engine finally sputtered to life.

Snow jumped back as I reversed and then drove out of the lot quickly. The road was clear, it was the middle of Nowhere after all, and I drove off.

Once at a safe distance, I found a spot to pull over and call Sick.

"Hello," I said, "I may have just quit slash been fired slash stolen a sheep slash rescued a friend slash co-worker; can I get shelter somewhere?"

CHAPTER 18

I had gotten to the safe house with no issues; Dr. Calamity was informed and she was already making a remedy treatment for Mary.

It was one level, small thing, just a bedroom, a living room, and a small kitchen/dining room area. Very empty with sparse furniture but enough to be serviceable.

"Ok, bit impulsive," said Sick, "I absolutely understand why you did that, and I am thankful that it didn't happen to you. I would have preferred you not making such a mess of this but if it happened to her, it could have happened to you."

"I think there is a but coming," I said.

"Why would you think that?"

"Because there is always a big, stinky but coming."

"In this case, the but is that you did, technically, steal someone's property, while I believe you in that this sheep was and is a person, named Mary, and that helping her was the right thing to do, someone else may disagree. If someone didn't buy your version of events, they could legally try to arrest you and return the sheep to its rightful..." he then used air quotes for the next word "'owner', so not an ideal situation."

"I see." I felt a knot in my stomach... or maybe that is what I had for lunch... I knew I should not have ordered from Quick Licks.

Then Sue burst into the room. "I have a plan," she said with the kind of glee that I would expect of a woman whose husband told her that he would do anything to make her happy, and she had just realized that "Anything" included the chores he had been neglecting.

"What is your battle plan?" asked Sick.

"In order to repossess the sheep, they have to be able to prove that they own it, they might try to fake it but that would result in a mess of paperwork. If they try to come without that they would be doing it illegally."

"Assuming that they didn't just ignore all that," I said.

I then got to see the sight of Sue deflating like a balloon.

"Actually, we may be able to modify that," said Sick.

He got out his cell phone and then put it away again. His next act was to stand up and leave the house locking the door behind him. However, after locking it, he immediately un-locked it and popped his head in for a moment.

"If I am not back in thirty minutes assume the worst." Then he reclosed and actually locked the door, for real this time.

Twenty minutes later he was back.

"I called the other officer, the guy you spoke to yesterday, Lou Tenant, he has promised that if this comes across his desk, he will be a stickler for the rules, should buy us a few days."

"How long until the treatment for Mary arrives?" asked Sue.

"A few days," I said.

"I see the problem," said Sue.

I looked over at Mary who was gently nudging my thigh.

"What do you need? Can you walk me to it?"

Mary nodded and I followed her to the back door.

"Food or bathroom?" said Sue, "One stomp for food, two for bathroom."

Two stomps.

"In the name of not giving away that we have a sheep to our neighbors, I am going to suggest you go in the bathtub, follow me," said Sue. Mary did. "Hope you like going grungy because this place is going to STINK."

"I will order some supplies," said Sick, "Should allow us to keep Mary inside until the medicine arrives."

I sat back to look forward to a long few, smelly days.

The supplies, mostly hay and bleach for the tub, arrived that evening and we all had dinner. Lou texted us saying all was quiet. Sick suggested booting up Immoral Combat, so we did and Sue kicked both of our butts while Mary watched. The last important thing was that Dr. Calamity texted us saying that the treatment for Mary was on the way, and should arrive in three more days.

The next day was also quiet, even though we took turns dousing the bathtub with bleach after Mary used it, the smell was starting to get intense. Not everything went down the drain when Mary used it and the smell of bleach mixed with the smell of urine and feces, was not a pleasant smell. Mary herself did not smell the best either, the cramped conditions of animals, or people, back at Sodom Hill probably did not lend itself to cleanliness. In short, the safe house began to reek. To make it worse, it was a small house, with one bedroom, used by Sick and Sue. One bathroom, which we used for everything but bathing, that connected through the bedroom, meaning you had to go through where Sick and Sue were sleeping to make a midnight bathroom break. The living room, which is where Mary and I slept, I got the couch, and she got a chair, was right next to the front door. A joint kitchen and dining area connected to the living room. And a hallway connecting the living room to the bedroom and bathroom.

The only good news was that the place had A.C. The bad news was that given how early into summer it was, and how hot it already was outside, we really needed the A.C and going for a walk to get out of the smell was dangerous even if you weren't hiding from a madman who turns people into sheep in order to make a profit.

To make myself less bored I made a way for Mary to talk to us. It was simply a board with letters on it that she could use to spell out words, basically a keyboard/ Ouija Board, but it worked for us to have some conversations.

Day two… not counting the day I arrived, was also quiet and smelly, body odor from humans started to add to the stink. We had grown tired of the endless violence of Immoral Combat and switched it up to Monopolizing. We had even found a way for Mary to play that, using nods, headshakes, and feet stomping to get her ideas across. Combined with the keyboard and patience she could even make trades, build hotels, all that good stuff. Granted Monopolizing is a tortuous game even under the best circumstances, but this way she could suffer with us and experience some of our pain.

Day three, with the treatment to make Mary human again arriving tomorrow, hopes were looking up. We had not had any trouble so far, which just made Sick more suspicious that something was wrong.

"There is no way it is this easy," he said.

"What if it was?" asked Sue.

"Then our enemy is incompetent," said Sick. "This would look cut and dry if you didn't know about the animal transformation stuff. Trixie stole a sheep, arrest her and return the sheep to its owners. What are we going to do, if I told you that this sheep was once a person, and you only knew what we knew last year, would you believe me?"

"They might be unable to provide paperwork that the sheep is legally his," said Sue. "Maybe Lou Tenant is covering for us."

"Maybe, but why wouldn't he say that? Why would he say all is well or all is quiet when he is running a desperate interception? Last night he texted me that no one had done anything about this, no complaints, no reports, nothing. The only thing he is concerned about is a missing person's report on Trixie, filed by your neighbor."

"Filed by Trip?" I asked.

"Yeah," said Sick, "If it weren't for this situation, I would text him saying that you're OK, as it is, I feel like it is all too easy."

Despite Sick's concerns the only thing keeping me up at night was the smell.

Then day four arrived, our salvation was at hand, and so was Mary's. The package was scheduled to arrive at four PM That was when the delivery driver was supposed to drop it off, but four PM came and went and there was no package. The concerns grew when Dr. Calamity texted us saying she was told the package had been shipped.

"I knew it," said Sick, "Someone figured it out."

"But how?" asked Sue.

"Any operation that could brew up that concoction would have some serious resources behind it. Trixie, you said that Dr. Calamity has special equipment to brew that stuff, right?"

"Yes," I said.

"Then in order to make something similar, these illegal operations have to have their own version of it that would require some level of sophistication, with these resources you might also be able to track people. The bug weed interceptions, that would take some level of skill and man power, you might have to have the kind of criminal empire that could monitor a small town such as this to the point where you would know everything."

"I thought that everyone knew everyone else's business in a small town anyway?" said Sue.

"Which just makes it worse," said Sick, "Any rumors could be overheard, we could be…"

Sick was interrupted by the doorbell.

He looked to the door and then back at us "Hide everyone, hide."

We did. Mary and I hid behind the couch, Sue crouched behind the chair. Sick, after checking that he had his pistol, went to the door.

After a moment of tension, the door creaked open.

"Howdy," said the woman at the door, "I think this got delivered to me by mistake."

"Uhh… let me see… Yes, that is ours," said Sick.

"Here you go then," said the woman.

"Um… Thanks," said Sick.

"Anytime," said the woman, walking away.

Sick returned to the living room, we all came out of hiding and Sick opened up the box. Inside I saw a large thermos. Sick handed the thermos to me and I looked inside. Inside the thermos was liquid nitrogen, and inside that was a smaller thermos. I brought the large thermos to the table and carefully removed the small thermos. Inside was a cold but not freezing tamper-proof vial of what looked like our solution.

"That is the stuff," I said.

"Have I really been panicking over nothing?" asked Sick.

"Maybe," said Sue, "It is one of your many qualities."

I looked at one of the plastic vials and the solution looked good.

"I think we are ready," I said and went off to the bedroom with Mary following closely behind.

"Ok Mary, you just have to drink this," I said opening up the vial and letting her lap up the solution. When it was all down her throat the waiting began.

"I will check in on you in an hour OK?" I said to Mary.

Mary said baaaaa and shook her head.

"Hold on," I said, and I ran out to grab the keyboard.

When I got back I put the keyboard down in front of Mary "What do you want?" I asked.

She typed out, "TRIXIE-PLEASE-STAY."

I sighed, looked at her, and said "OK."

And so I stayed with her; to be fair she was probably very frightened. I know I was back when it was my turn.

It was an all-night ordeal. In the end, we both fell asleep in the bedroom, but by that time her hooves looked very different, almost like hands and feet. The face somehow looked a bit like Mary now, I could actually see her in that face, not just a strange-looking sheep.

In the morning I woke up at sunrise and saw that Mary was now fully human, tucked into a blanket on the floor, on top of a mat next to the bed.

I walked out to tell Sue and Sick and found that they were both asleep in the living room on the floor and that the clocks told me it was only five AM.

"What's up." Said Sue groggily

"Oh, Mary is human again," I whispered.

"What… Mary is human again." Sue yawned and curled back up to Sick under the blanket. "That's nice," she said.

Before I could figure out what happened, Sue Jolted back up. "MARY IS HUMAN AGAIN!" This jolted Sick awake and Sue suddenly raced past me to the master bedroom.

Once everyone was up there was a scramble. Mary didn't have any clothes with her so she wore a towel.

"I should get her something to wear," said Sick.

"Do you even know what a woman needs?" asked Sue. "I can get her clothing,"

"What should I do then, wait outside?"

"If you like."

I looked to Mary, "You feeling OK?"

"I don't know," she said. "I feel exposed now. I did as a sheep, but I got used to it, but now I am not sure… on the plus side, I think my boobs went up a size."

"Let me measure to make sure," said Sue.

"Is it OK if I ask Trixie to do the measurements instead?"

"Trixie you up for it?"

"I can handle it," I said only somewhat lying.

A few way too long and way too awkward minutes in the bedroom with a tape measure later and we had our answer. She had indeed gone up two sizes.

Upon hearing the news, she was dancing, quite happy about it.

"I got a buff, I got a buff…" said Mary with a giddy smile, "No longer just average."

"Meaning you will have to replace all your bras," I said, "Bet that will be a chore."

"Who cares… look I'm almost as big as you now."

I rolled my eyes and threw the towel back at her.

After sending Sue on her merry way, Sick made a final scrub of the bathtub. Now it was finally safe to actually take a shower in. Sick was first, then Mary, then myself. Though I waited an extra half hour for the heater to make hot water again.

When I got out Sue had gotten back with a few outfits for Mary. They were plain, boring, and other words to describe clothing a fashionista wouldn't be caught dead in, but Mary didn't care, she seemed happy to be wearing clothes and not carrying a towel with her everywhere. Sue took a shower while Mary changed and then we were off to the races. We had way too many things to do, and approximately not enough time to do them all. The first order of business was to visit Officer Lou Tenant.

"Hello Mary and Trixie, good to see you are safe, I can revoke those missing person reports."

"Do I have one?" asked Mary.

"Yeah," said Lou, "I filed it when Trixie went missing, and I couldn't reach you."

"Sorry about that," said Sick, "Something happened, I had to keep them with me for a few days. Out of curiosity, can you check this wool sample for DNA?"

"Sure," said Lou, "May I ask why?"

"Because this wool came from this young woman," he said pointing to Mary. "I also have pictures."

"That's… quite a claim."

Sick handed Lou a big notebook. Lou opened it up.

"Strange," said Lou, flipping through the pages.

"I know it is a lot to take in."

"No… I mean… that guy Richard… sorry," Lou snickered. "Dick from B.O.O.B., he rambled for a few minutes about some secret government program to turn horses into people… then got mad that no one wanted to sign his non-disclosure agreement after he told us.”

“He did that to you too?” I asked.

“What did I miss?” asked Mary.

“It's a long story,” I said.

“Not really,” said Lou. “Just apparently the government once thought that turning horses into people was a good idea, it didn't work out, even though apparently, they made the process itself work. I laughed him out of the building… but now… broken clock right twice a day and all.

“Anyhow, the important part is that I can close out these missing person reports, let Trip know you are alright, and then figure out what to do about Snow… I am sure you will tell me more about the whole horse people thing, right?”

“More like sheep for now,” said Sick. He turned to Mary, “Can I show him?”

“Go for it,” said Mary sitting down.

“I have this video,” said Sick. “It will help us.

He then showed Sick a video of Mary as a sheep, tapping out answers to his questions on the keyboard I made.

“What is your name?” said Sick in the video.

Mary then typed out the letters on the board and Sue spoke for her.

“Mary.”

“Were you human?”

“Yes.”

“When did you become a sheep?”

“Two days ago.”

“How did that happen?”

“Snow Leatherfall must have slipped something into my water… I arrived early because he asked me to do some silly thing. I left my water just outside the lab, he must have tampered with it."

"Ok… That took a while. Last question… I don't… Do you know why Mr. Leatherfall did this?"

"No."

Back in the real-world Lou looked shocked.

"I…I," he stammered.

"Sorry about the long part," said Mary.

"Normally this wouldn't mean anything… but there is an unrelated charge to Leatherfall. His cousin who runs… ran the local police until yesterday is being charged with corruption, and some complaints about Leatherfall came up. I have a warrant to search Sodom Hill, I can do that today… you down to go with? I could use some people with me who know the place."

"I am, don't know about these two," said Sick, gesturing to us.

I was tired and ready to get out and go home. I had done all I was asked and was ready to actually start my life, so I was going to say no.

Yet the words that came out of my mouth were, "Yes I'm in."

"If nothing else, I would like to at least try and recover my cellphone, I couldn't remember my passwords to report them as stolen," said Mary. "Also might give me some closure."

Well, too late for me to back out now.

Back at Sodom Hill, it was quiet. We went to the trash can that had Mary's phone in it. A very kind officer, wearing gloves, searched the trash can, and found that her phone was destroyed, likely something heavy was thrown on it and the thing was shattered into pieces.

The most concerning thing to me was, well, I looked out the back. All the sheep were gone.

"If they are all like Mary, and I think they are, then that is a lot of missing people."

"Under the assumption that you are right, how many sheep were there?" asked Lou.

I shrugged, "I don't know, a lot… I never counted."

"I am now hoping you are wrong," said Lou.

Another officer approached me, "Um… Ms. Night do you know a Stuck?"

"Stuck Holms? Yes, why?" I said, turning to face him.

"We found him tied up in a back room… looks like he has been there a while."

We ran to go find him and yep he was a mess, crying, and drinking water.

"Trixie! He shouted suddenly, standing up. "You're alright!"

Several officers tried to get him to sit down again.

"I'm fine," I said, "You look worse for wear."

"I never saw that coming from Snow… I thought he was an OK guy?" Stuck started to sob.

I saw a car pull up and Trip popped out. He locked eyes with me and seemed to breathe a sigh of relief.

"Um, sir," said an officer.

"I was told to come here by officer Tenant," said Trip. "Though I mostly wanted to check that a neighbor of mine was alright, I can leave if you…"

"Let him in," said Lou.

The other officer nodded and waved Trip in.

"Is everyone OK officer Tenant?" Trip asked.

"You can call me Lou… and mixed results on everyone OK. Trixie here is OK, we found Mary, she was with her…

though no one submitted a missing person report for her. Save for myself when I couldn't get in touch after Trixie was reported missing." He turned to Mary, "Sorry about that."

"It's OK," said Mary. "I had just moved here and… no one knew to check on me… my parents probably don't care."

"We did try to reach them," said Lou. "I will tell you about it later."

"Did they say I was dead to them?"

Lou looked around wincing before looking down with a sigh, "Yes… they said that… exactly."

"I thought I was having a bad day," said Stuck.

Lou sighed, "You are, you're having a bad day. Mary is having a bad day. I suspect in a moment Trip will be having a bad day. Everyone is having a bad day. It's not a competition."

"What about me?" asked Trip, "Is something wrong?"

"We think your father may have kidnapped people. At the very least Stuck's testimony suggests that he absolutely did."

"Oh my god."

"I know it's a lot to take in."

"Mostly I didn't think he had that kind of… will to do it."

"How do you mean?"

"Everything I know about my father. The bad thing about him is that he was so used to getting his way that when we tried to balance for fairness, he would throw a tantrum. But when challenged he was bluffing almost every time, and might end up begging people to change their minds and giving them what they wanted."

"Working for him was like that," I said, "He would call you and demand you come in on a day off, but back down if you threatened to quit over it."

"How long did it take you to figure that out?" asked Lou.

"Before I started working," I said. "It was the weekend before. I hadn't started and he demanded I come in, backed down when I threatened to quit, honestly not sure why I agreed to come back."

"I also learned that," said Mary. "Tried to get me to come in the weekend before I was supposed to start. I was an all-day drive away at the time. Quit on the spot and he spent the next day begging me to reconsider."

"Odd," said Lou. "This man does not sound like a criminal genius, yet he was able to keep you out of the loop."

"We believe he had help," said Sick. "Some of the stuff going on here was linked to another location."

Lou thought for a moment, pacing back and forth.

"Trip," Lou said finally.

"Yes," said Trip.

"How much contact do you have with your father?"

"I haven't spoken to him in half a year."

"Sick, when did the stuff with the previous operation go down?"

"Almost one year ago," said Sick.

"Ok then back to Trip," said Lou. "Describe how things went down normally at this place, do you know?"

"Not much," said Trip. "Not like what they would know at least. I just helped with animal feeding."

Lou turned to look at Stuck.

"He did; left after a few months."

"How did he help you?" asked Lou.

"He covered the weekends and assisted every day except Wednesday and Thursday," said Stuck.

"What happened when Trip left?"

"Snow got someone else to replace him."

"But you have been working alone?"

"For most of the past year, yeah."

"Now Stuck, the lab, do you know how many people worked it?"

"Used to be at least four on any given day. But now he was down to ones and twos."

Lou turned to Trip.

"As far as I know that's right for when I worked here," said Trip. "Four on any one day, no one on weekends."

Then Lou turned to Mary and me.

"It was just us," I said, "and before Mary, it was just me. I replaced the previous guy who left on my first day."

"Did you get his name?" asked Lou.

"Justin, Justin Time."

"I will have someone look for him… in the meantime," Lou turned to Stuck, "did the lab experience a sudden loss of workers at some point?"

"It did," said Stuck, "Not all at once. About a year ago Snow just stopped replacing the people who quit until there was almost no one left."

"So can we agree that based on all of this?" said Lou generally, "That Snow's performance dropped suddenly when the other place was investigated? Almost a year ago?"

There was a general amount of nodding.

"Then Snow had help from there, it got cut off, leaving him nothing but his own bad decision-making."

"You think that he was reliant on outside help?" asked Mary.

"It makes sense," said Lou, "The similar operation that Sick, Sue, and Trixie disrupted, the timing from what we know… in general this operation was completely unsustainable… I would give it another half a year before collapsing on its own… so Snow just ran away… probably the only smart decision he could make."

Sick raised his hand, "Um… sorry this is well and good, and the other operation was turning people into sheep…"

"Wait, WHAT?" shouted Stuck.

Mary turned to him, "It happened to me, we have photos."

Lou turned to an officer, "Get Mister Stuck up to speed please."

The officer nodded and gently guided Stuck away.

Lou tuned to Sick, "You were saying?"

"Right… If the same thing was happening here, and we think it might have been… then … all the missing sheep are people… where are they… where did Snow run too… does he have the sheep/people, and are they in any danger?"

Lou nodded, "Those are all very good questions that we don't have answers for."

CHAPTER 19

We had a general meeting with myself, Lou, Sick, Sue, Mary, and Dr. Calamity, coming in remotely.

"So the good news," said Lou. "Is we found a huge amount of all sorts of contraband at Sodom Hill and based on Trixie, Mary, Stuck, Justin, and other witnesses, as well as the location of said contraband, only Snow could have been messing with the stuff. We have one target; the question is where would he go?"

There was a knock on the door and officer Lou let in Trip.

"Sorry, I'm late," he said.

"No problem," said Lou. "You did let me know by text… just as long as you stopped to do that."

"I had to mess with my GPS anyway," said Trip. "So either I was stupid enough to do both on the road and probably die, or I stopped at a Melon's restaurant parking lot to turn around."

Lou nodded, "Well you missed almost nothing… anyway, does anyone have any ideas where Snow would have gone? Or how we could find him."

"If he tries to sell the sheep, there should already be a bit of a moratorium in place," said Sue. "If he does, this might pop up on some legal frequency."

"There was some memo about some sheep sold illegally," said Lou. "Snow's did match the description, I can send out another memo, hopefully, someone sees them. But I need to know where Snow might try to head."

"He used to 'joke' about disappearing to the big city when mom or I annoyed him," said Trip. "Never said which city. He also used to try to tell me that if I ever got in trouble with the police the first thing that I do is to drain my account and take cash with me for everything. So he probably would have drained his account and then used cash for everything."

Lou nodded, "Then he might be invisible… what could we do to find him?"

"He does yell and complain a lot," said Trip. "He might get in trouble somehow."

"What about the sheep?" asked Sick.

"They are smart," I said. "They might be able to signal for help… if he is traveling with them, then that is a lot of sheep."

"I could remember a lot about being a human when I was transformed," said Mary. "They can probably remember being kidnapped, and everything… so they might be able to signal for help."

"As long as they are still alive… and that he is carrying them… who knows."

"I may have a secret tool," said Lou. "Not a great tool, but if we are desperate… For now, I will put out posters to keep an eye out for the strange sheep. Also, I hear that Trixie and Mary need to get Mary her life set up again… good luck."

So we were excused and Mary and I hopped in Hank to make the hour-long drive to the local mall.

"I would like to ask you something," I said.

"Go ahead," said Mary.

"This is a bit personal for me… but I… was also transformed into a sheep at one point."

It was a bit hard to say… just because I hadn't really talked about it with anyone for a while… not really since telling Sue about it for that court case.

"It sucks I know," said Mary. "Believe me I know."

"Right… but I had some questions… in my experience, I can't remember much, what I do remember is that I couldn't remember anything."

"How do you mean?"

"I know I was drawing blanks on names and faces… and my experience was a blur."

"I have a few gaps," said Mary. "But after the first few hours I remember things clearly, I couldn't picture your face… but when I saw you, I knew it was you… it was like I suddenly remembered that you were a friend of mine, and that you could help me."

I nodded while keeping my eyes on the road.

"Mine was a lot shorter than yours…" I said. "I was back to human the next day… it was a lab accident and my professor was able to make the antidote that evening. Maybe memories are lost in the transition… or rather memories of the transition are lost."

"That would make some sense," said Mary. "My biggest blanks are just before changing the first time, and changing back."

There was an awkward-feeling silence in the car after this.

"We're like our own little support group," said Mary. "Just the two of us… hopefully with more soon."

"I… maybe," I said. "I think that in the other major group of this… *Leaf It To Me*, that the victims did form their own support group afterward."

"That was that farm that was caught human trafficking. They did this too?" said Mary. "Maybe you should join them."

"I wasn't kidnapped like they were, I was only for one day, didn't feel like I belonged."

"I see… want to change the subject?"

We talked about random things for a bit, then Mary found a radio station playing country songs, turned it off, tried finding anything else, then found news, which was all about the crazy sheep farm so she gave up and turned the radio off. She then wanted to play music on her phone before remembering that her phone was in a police station and in pieces. She gave up and I glanced over, seeing her looking out a window as my phone didn't have any music.

We finally got to Everbrock, found the mall, and started shopping.

"Mind if we look in the men's sections first," said Mary. "I want pants with real pockets, not the fake ones that they sew shut for some reason in women's pants."

"I get my pants from the men's section as well," I admitted. "In fact the last time I was in the woman's section it was to buy a formal dress that I wore exactly once."

So we started getting clothes, then Mary's new phone, then listened to Mary rant for half an hour about how the model she wanted was no longer being sold, and that all the new ones have different chargers, and how stupid it was to make the charger port and headphone port the same port. She switched from a Peachtree phone to a Robo-teck phone which at least still had separate charge and headphone ports.

Then we got some dinner at the food court. Mary quietly admitted to me that she was vegan, blushing the whole time, it was adorable. We made our way back to Hank with our haul. Just as soon as we got out of the building a whole herd of Sapi sheep showed up. Baaing like crazy.

"Hold on… That's them… the other sheep from Sodom Hill," said Mary.

"You sure?" I asked, already getting Lou out in my contacts list.

"Yes… I can't say how I know… I don't know how I know… but it… I just know you know… like how I knew you when I was…"

"Got it," I said, dialing Lou. "Hello Lou, you are not going to believe this."

"Is this a good 'you're not going to believe this', or a bad 'you're not going to believe this?'" asked Lou.

"Good," I said.

Lou sighed, "Thank God for that… I am having enough trouble tracking down an entire herd of Sapi sheep I could use some good news."

"Funny you should mention that," I said.

CHAPTER 20

The next day I was talking with Sick.

"So how are things?" I asked.

"Calamity is coming back from Dedlam to turn our sheep back into humans, Lou has confirmed their humanness, some have even given us names that match missing persons reports. Mary is also doing well, she is getting all of her accounts sorted out right now, and we are thinking that you may want to take a week or two off."

"Sounds nice," I said.

"Right, we just got a few things to do and then hopefully you will have done your part. We have a line out on Snow, so hopefully that is all we need you for. Though I think I might want to keep you on in case anything similar shows up," said Sick.

I nodded, this all sounded great, then Lou came in looking like he was about to strangle someone.

"Idiots," said Lou with a quiet rage that frightened me to the core. "This entire department is made up of idiots... and all the departments within one hundred miles, all of them, idiots."

"How do you…" began Sick.

"They couldn't track an entire herd of sheep," said Lou, without raising his voice an octave. "A bunch of country boys, many of whom grew up hunting and on farms, couldn't track an entire herd of sheep. A herd of smart sheep, that probably wanted to be found based on how they walked to a mall parking lot. I am wondering if any of them could pour water out of a boot… with instructions on how to do so written on the heel."

There was a knock on the door.

"Come in," growled Lou.

The door opened and a nervous-looking officer stepped in. "Um… Sir," he said, "We have a problem."

Lou rolled his eyes, "What is it this time?"

"Um… We spoke with Stuck… from Sodom Hill… he said that he had a record of how many sheep he was tending for… the last update, from the day he was locked up, was two hundred and fifty-six."

"How many do we have?" said Lou.

"We have just ninety-eight," said the officer.

"Hold on, let me do some math," said Lou, bringing out his phone. "Stupid calculator app." He sighed, "Ok Goober, what is two hundred and fifty-six minus ninety-eight?"

Goober answered, "The number is one hundred and fifty-eight."

"Thank you, Goober," Lou stood up. "So, we have one hundred and fifty-eight sheep missing."

The officer scratched the back of his head, "Well… yes."

"See if you and your department can redeem yourselves… find them."

The officer ran out of the office we were in.

Lou sighed again, then turned to us, "So what do we do when they inevitably fail."

"Talk to the soon-to-be people… sheep, to be people…?" I suggested.

"They might know something," said Sick. "Mary seems to have some memory of what happened, maybe they will know where the rest went."

Lou nodded, "And then we will need to find Snow. Otherwise, he might try this with some other group of people."

The next few days were quiet, then Calamity arrived and I helped her set up the treatment, or rather we did ninety percent of the work because the guys the police department sent over were… completely useless, just as Lou predicted.

On the second day, Mary came to help and we got a lot more done with three people than we ever would with two. Work continued and we managed to get enough treatment for all the sheep after three days of work.

Once the last sheep was back to human, we had another meeting.

"Good job you two," started Calamity, gesturing to myself and Mary. "Probably would have taken all week without you."

"Glad that some people here are useful," said Lou. "Unfortunately the three of you may be it. Seriously I have about fifty meetings about corruption searches in what is now my department, that I am now in charge of. Meanwhile, everyone else is either doing routine work, traffic stops, speeding tickets, that sort of thing, or working on this one case. And the only two things they have contributed are one, a headcount of sheep, and two doing some interviews… I have been listening to recordings of said interviews by the way. Do you know how many officers missed the victims describing a livestock truck?"

"How many?" asked Sick.

"Every single one of them," said Lou. "I have a very solid description out but I had to do it myself, had to talk to the officers again… One of them admitted that the previous boss,

Richard Bent, never had them do much outside of traffic stops."

Lou sighed and slouched in his chair, "We have twice the number of officers we need for traffic stops, using a generous estimate of how many we need, and still have speeding and drunk driving problems in the area. Anyways back to the topic… the livestock trailer is a common model, nowhere near enough to handle the missing one hundred and fifty-eight."

"What did the victims say happened?" asked Sue.

"They tell us that they broke out of the enclosure, and then traveled along, some say that they split the herd at one point, and then found their way into the city."

Trip suddenly piped up, in the process reminding everyone he was there.

"Can these people tell us about where it happened? My father used to take me hunting; I can track an animal."

"The officers under me said it was impossible… if you show them up I would either be impressed with you or un-impressed with them. Let's see what happens," said Lou.

By the end of the day, Trip had somehow found fifty-nine of the missing sheep people, they were hiding in a cave.

Then Dick from B.O.O.B. showed up.

"I want all the sheep you have, they are government intellectual property," screamed Dick into Lou's face.

Lou wiped the spit from his face, "I don't know that we can do that."

"YES YOU CAN, YOU HAVE TO," screamed Dick.

Lou shook his head.

"AS A GOVERNMENT AGENT…."

Lou extended a handout, "Warrant?" he asked.

"I WILL… what?" said Dick from B.O.O.B.

"Do you have a warrant for their transfer? Right now they are evidence in a case, and also witnesses. If you cannot provide me a warrant for their transfer into your custody, then I cannot let you take them."

"He is right," said Sue. "There is a moratorium on these sheep, they are considered stolen until the law catches up and declares them kidnapped." She looked at her fingernails. "They cannot legally give them to you… unless you can provide documentation that they are yours, and we can get either get a judge to sign off that either they are no longer useful as evidence, or that you can provide proof that you will treat them properly as evidence."

Dick huffed, "Give them to me right NOW!"

"No," said Lou, "Now please leave."

"Or…" said Dick with the kind of smirk only seen on kids who think they have outsmarted a parent or teacher.

Lou turned to Sue, "As a lawyer, what would you do in this situation?"

"Depends, am I a scumbag lawyer or a bloodthirsty shark lawyer?" asked Sue.

Lou stared.

Sick stood up, "I got this. I know my Wife." He turned to Sue, "What would you do as a scumbag lawyer?"

Sue smiled, "Run circles around everyone for two years, making every step hurt before eventually coming to an agreement with Dick from B.O.O.B."

"In two years we will have all these sheep back into people," said Sick. "And they will likely either be in witness protection or running free."

"They could be free-range yes," said Sue.

"What about as a bloodthirsty shark?" asked Lou.

Sue glanced down, the shadow of her brow over her eyes made her look a bit like an over-the-top villain. "Dick is interrupting an important case, in which human trafficking is involved, he is threatening to delay innocent people returning to their daily lives. He is arguably preventing us from getting important work done, thereby this is obstruction of justice. No jury would have a qualm of charging him."

Dick glared at Sue, "But you forget you stupid hag, that I work for the government."

Sue cocked her head at Dick, "As I said, no jury would have a qualm of charging you."

Sue changed her position, "Of course by that point they will be back to human. Actually how much longer... Dr. Calamity, how much longer until these sheep are people?"

"We made some extra, so some will be back to normal by midnight," said Calamity. "For the rest, it might take a day or two to get the treatment ready, but not much longer after that."

"So if Dick were to demand them back as evidence... would that mean he considers them property?"

"I don't know, you're the lawyer?"

"No, I'm the bloodthirsty shark lawyer, I can spin this as human trafficking, slavery."

"WHAT'S SO WRONG ABOUT BEING A SLAVE OWNER?" asked Dick.

I was shocked, not only that anyone actually said that out loud, but worse, he did it in a room that had Lou, clearly African American, in it.

Lou took several deep breaths, "Let me escort you out of my base."

"No," said Dick.

"Then I hereby charge you with trespassing, and will arrest you."

Dick moved to punch Lou, and hit him square in the face. Lou responded by putting Dick on the floor and wrestling him to the ground.

"You have the right to remain silent," said Lou to Dick once he had pinned Dick to the floor.

"YOU CAN'T DO THIS TO ME AGAIN," screamed Dick.

Lou sighed as he put handcuffs on Dick, "You have the right to an attorney, if you cannot afford one…"

"UN-HAND ME YOU PIECE OF…." Dick then said several words that I do not wish to repeat, especially given how they were directed toward a Black guy.

All this screaming gave me a headache so I turned away from the scene, then noticed a camera above Lou's desk. So hopefully this would keep him in jail.

Over the next few days, things were dull, making treatment to get sheep back into people. A general search was ordered. Trip lead it and they got back all but thirty-eight of the missing people who were transformed into sheep.

I was delivering the final batch of treatment, which would be enough for the rest of the people we had, and if preserved, enough for the ones we did not have.

"And you haven't spoken to her in a year?" said Lou to Trip.

Trip shook his head.

Lou turned to me, "Trixie, welcome, how is the lab going?"

"I am just putting these in the freezer, hopefully, they will be enough for the rest," I said.

Lou nodded and I continued to the freezer in the next room. Then I turned back to help clean up the lab.

Calamity, Mary, and I washed the test tubes, put everything back where we found it, except for one beaker that was now a pile of broken glass in a trashcan, and moved to leave.

Then we saw Lou, "I'm sorry guys" he began. "But I think I need you for something else."

"What is it?" I asked, "I'm not saying yes but…"

"I need some help to look over Ms. Leatherfall's place," said Lou. "Trip says that she and his father were on bad terms apparently, though they are still married and in the same house. We think that she is still residing there."

"So… what do I have to do with this?"

"If she is in on Snow's plans, then we will need someone who knows what to look for. That is you, Mary, and Calamity as we don't have anyone nearby who has even the slightest idea of how this works."

"I see," I said.

"If you can do it, then come by tomorrow morning, we should have a warrant by then."

"Why do we not have one now?" asked Trip.

"Paperwork, bureaucracy, you know," said Lou.

Trip nodded, and everyone went home.

Next morning was a little busy and we arrived at Trip's childhood home. The officers went in first, Trip's mother Autumn, was brought out. Sue began to talk to Autumn. Eventually Trip, Calamity, Mary and I were brought in to see if the officers missed anything. They hadn't, as far as we could tell, there was nothing lab-like there.

Walking out, there was a scene.

"Trip," said Autumn.

Trip said nothing and ignored her.

"I… I'm sorry," said Autumn.

Trip turned around and looked at her.

"Go on," he said.

Autumn looked to the ground, "For everything… for… shredding the college letters… and the books… and for destroying your music, spending your inheritance from your uncle, and also for… for screaming at you when you… told me you had… a… boyfriend."

She looked down and started to cry. "I screwed up, I had one chance and I screwed up. I… didn't want to… I thought… I just wanted to do what my parents taught me to do, what my church taught me to do, what my husband wanted me to do… I didn't think any of it through."

Trip sighed, "Better late than never."

"Do you forgive me?" Autumn asked.

Trip looked at her then shook his head.

Autumn started to cry, and fell to her knees.

"Not yet," said Trip, "Prove you're sorry."

Autumn looked to him, "How?"

"You said you didn't think any of it through… Start thinking things through now."

Trip then walked away.

Autumn turned to Sue, "When you see TV shows it is so easy, just one I'm sorry and it's all better."

Sue sighed, "This isn't a TV show," she said.

"I know… I don't care what you do to me… but keep my son safe, and put… the bastard I called a husband in jail. Then I can be happy."

"I will help you find a good local lawyer," said Sue. "I can't vouch for you but someone has to."

"The only people who need lawyers are guilty, and cowards," said Autumn. "What my husband always said… OK good point."

I decide to talk to Trip instead of listening in on this.

"So ummm…" I began.

"I am gay," said Trip. "Hope that's not a problem."

"No," I said. "I didn't suspect… you OK?"

"Hu… oh I'm fine…" he sighed, "Mom and Dad forced me to break up with my boyfriend when they found out. We are getting back together now, but… it has taken time. That was a hard lesson for me to learn. If mom can learn it… maybe someday."

I nodded, noting that I never had this particular problem in life.

They did find some notes, ultimately they included messages to and from *Leaf It To Me*, pictures of most of the people involved there, including Jay and his father, and a few phone numbers, most of which were *Leaf It To Me* related. We had just about given up when something happened on Friday, by chance.

It was another long and fruitless day, and I had just gone shopping for groceries. I was still at the apartment. I was about to make the first load when a car pulled up next to mine. Jay Walker hopped out of it. I took a step back almost immediately.

"Witch you are coming with me," he said.

"No," I said, dropping my groceries and running away.

"Get your butt back here you witch," said Jay, running behind me.

I decided better safe than sorry and blew my rape whistle.

"That won't save you," shouted Jay. "For what you did you will be coming with me and I will be having a great time hearing you scream."

Well he has gone off the deep end. I was hoping I could put some distance on him, just enough to unlock my apartment door, hop in, and close/lock it before he could reach me, but, as I climbed the stairs he was right behind me, I was sprinting, but needed to run this as a marathon… but slowing down was not an option, maybe I could trip him or something but… how I might have to run loops, that was possible as the apartment has stairs on both sides but… there was a loud thud behind me and an unfamiliar voice.

"Leave her alone," said the voice.

I glanced behind me and saw Jay suddenly on his back with a bloody nose. I stopped and turned around hoping my rescuer was just going to be a legit rescuer, and not some guy who would demand something for having done the right thing. What I found was a man, looked early 20s, wearing only underwear. In his defense he had the body for it, he even had visible abs.

"You alright ma'am?" he asked.

"I am fine," I said. "Also don't ma'am me."

Then I heard Trip's voice, "Honey, a zip tie, police are on the way." I briefly saw Trip's bare torso, he also looked good for it.

"Thanks dear," said my rescuer, obviously Trip's boyfriend, so much for any rescue romance ideas my head had for a moment.

Anyhow, Trip's boyfriend/partner/whatever, moved on Jay with the zip tie. "First off… ma'am it's just how I was raised, so I hope you understand, and second, you were just being chased by this guy and me calling you ma'am is setting you off."

"So my priorities might be out of order," I said, "But the only people who get ma'amed are old, and I'm not old."

"No ma'am you aren't," said Trip's friend. "But until I have a name it will have to do."

"Trixie," I said. "Also do you have a name so that I can stop mentally referring to you as Trip's Boyfriend?"

"Know," said the rescuer, "John Know, with a K, as in I know something."

I nodded.

"Also I am Trip's fiancé as of…" John checked his non-existent watch, then glanced inside Trip's apartment, "An hour and a half ago."

"Congratulations," I said, trying to hide my bitterness that these two caring and handsome, (especially handsome while almost naked) guys were not getting it on with me, and instead with each other.

"Can this conversation wait until I am not tied to a handrail looking at some guy's half-naked ass," said Jay, blood still running out of his nose.

"You wouldn't be looking at my boy--- sorry, fiancé's amazing half-naked ass and listening to this conversation if you hadn't attacked my neighbor and friend. Also, the cops are on their way and I hear that one of them is a recent friend of mine so you have bigger problems than this right now," said Trip.

Trip stepped outside with some actual clothing thereby robbing me of more eye candy. "I can keep an eye on him if you want to step in John."

"Yeah I should probably get dressed," said John.

It was at this point that I remembered that I had groceries to pick up.

So I was able to run down and get the rest of my groceries out of Hank, find that my dozen eggs that I dropped had not broken, but the gallon of milk I bought had been broken, get everything put away, and my milk into another container, at which point we could then wait half an hour for the cops to show up.

Lou was the one who greeted us. "Sorry for the delay," he said. "But this department only really cares about people driving more than half a mile an hour above the speed limit, how the town pays its bills."

"Well the only person who is really hurt by this is this Jay fellow," said John.

"Sick and Sue might want to hear about this."

Lou sighed, "I am sure they will. Now if you will excuse me, I am supposed to be meeting my wife for dinner in fifteen minutes so if you three would like to make your statements tomorrow.

"Sure. That will give me time to download the doorbell," said Trip.

Lou looked at Trip like he had grown three heads.

"It's one with a camera," said Trip.

"Out here?" said Lou. "It's not exactly crime city here."

"Falling out with dad, you know how it is."

"I don't, but OK," said Lou.

He then got out a pair of hand cuffs.

"Now let's bag our guy."

We followed Lou up to the balcony.

"These people tied me to the balcony officer, you should be arresting them not me."

"We will see it on the doorbell camera," said Trip.

"There is no way you saw me attacking that bitch Trixie," said Jay.

Lou immediately face palmed. "A shame we won't be able to use that because I haven't read him his rights yet."

"But it's true, that camera won't be able to see me all the way down there."

"Sir," said Lou to Jay, "You have the right to remain silent."

"But she got me fired."

"Anything you say can, and will be used against you in a court of law."

"I only wanted to talk to her, I wasn't going to rape her or anything."

"You have the right to an attorney." By this point Lou had the regular cuffs on Jay and had cut the zip tie.

"She told Calamity to fire me I know it."

"If you cannot afford an attorney, one will be appointed for you."

"If I wanted to kill her, she would be dead."

Lou started man-handling Jay to the patrol car, "The point of why I said all of that is because you are supposed to realize that you should stop talking until the lawyer gets here. For this and other free tips try being polite and being quiet until you use your one phone call to get a lawyer."

There was a lot of commotion the next day.

Trip, Sue, John, Mary, Calamity and I were waiting for Lou and Sick to finish up.

John looked around, "So Dr. Calamity?"

She turned to him, "Yes?"

"I understand that you did some recent work with a gene treatment that changes the male to female ratios in some animals before birth."

"Yeah, that was just before Trixie came into my lab, what about it?"

"It helped my family out a lot," said John. "My dad owns a silk goat ranch… he said he will give it to me next year… so I wanted to thank one of the people responsible for keeping it profitable."

Calamity smiled, "Glad to have helped."

Lou and Sick came out of the interrogation room.

"Good news and bad news," said Lou. "The good news is we got some good stuff out of him, we even have a signed confession with his lawyer with us."

"The bad news," said Sick, "Is that he had a list, yes Trixie you were on the list… so was Mary… And also Justin. We will contact him and get his help… meanwhile, we need to get you to somewhere safe… and no we don't have a safe house."

"What about the place that you transformed me back to human?" asked Mary.

"Caught fire last night," said Sick.

"Fire men put it out," said Sue. "But it is not as much of a house anymore, and is certainly not safe."

John and Trip started whispering at each other, Trip nodded, and then John turned to us.

"My silk goat ranch is an hour away; would that be safe enough?"

Lou and Sick turned to each other, nodded to each other, then they turned to us. "Sure, it's probably our best bet."

"I will start packing," I said.

"We will be checking in every day starting tomorrow," said Lou. "So if you have anything illegal you have until tomorrow to get rid of it."

Trip and John nodded.

"Will someone be there at all hours?" asked Sick.

"Sure," said John. "I work from home, and based on our conversation Trip will be quitting his job soon to be my stay-at-home husband."

"Do you want me to pick you guys up?" asked Trip.

"I can drive," I said.

"I no longer have a car," said Mary.

"I can pick you up," I said before turning to John, "Just give me an address and I will let you know when we're on our way."

John nodded and found a piece of paper to write a phone number and address on.

After packing and picking up Mary we made the fifty-eight-minute drive to John's farm.

It was a large goat farm, stinking of manure, baa-ing, all that good stuff.

The silk goats were smaller than regular ones, I think. I'm not an expert. There was a large red barn, there was a path for the goats to go in and out of, a large tank and what looked like a lab building.

The main house was two stories old but well-maintained and brick. It had solar panels on its roof, and what looked like a small wind turbine. I couldn't help but wonder how John could afford such a place.

Mary and I grabbed our luggage and started toward the ranch.

"You two got everything?" asked John.

"I traveled here light," I said. "No offense but I don't want to stay here."

"I only got the essentials," said Mary.

John nodded and invited us inside.

"So Mary," said John, "Trixie told me you are vegan."

"I can get my own food if it's an issue," said Mary.

John laughed, "Do you mind false vegan."

"Meat plants?" asked Mary, "I'm fine with it."

"Then Trip will have dinner ready in half an hour. He is a good cook I promise."

He then started grabbing our stuff.

"As for sleeping arrangements, we have one guest room with a two-person bed in it. If you two are not comfortable sharing one bed, one of you can take the couch. You can fight over that position, alternate days, just let us know and we'll get you set up."

"I can take the couch," I volunteered.

"A… are you sure?" said Mary, "We can share a bed."

"Positive," I said. "No offence, but I would rather have a couch alone than share a bed with someone."

"What about the right someone?" she asked, with an obviously flirtatious look on her face.

"I don't think I have found them yet," I replied.

"I see."

We then went inside.

"Pardon the mess," said John on the way into a room that looked like it had been polished to a mirror shine. Like seriously, I wish I could have kept my one-room apartment half as clean as this entire house on a farm.

"Nice flexing," said Mary.

"Thanks," said John with a grin.

"Where is Trip?" I asked.

"Grocery shopping," said John, "I have to text him quickly so that he doesn't try to find vegan meat substitutes and just get the false vegan stuff. It's cheaper."

"Tell me about it," said Mary.

"How do you know about this?" I asked.

"I have a cousin who is vegetarian," said John. "And as much as he is my cousin and I love him for that… I wish we could get him to shut up about it."

"Don't worry," said Mary. "I don't need to remind everyone about it every three and a half nanoseconds."

"Good, we will get along then," said John as he turned to me. "Could you help me set up a couch for you?"

I nodded and walked with him.

"You know," he said, "I think Mary was trying to flirt with you back there."

"I figured," I said.

"Good," said John, "You made your decision, and I think you let her down gently. At least you weren't like me, not able to pick up on Trip practically throwing himself at me… when we were both in a gay bar."

I blinked a couple of times.

"I am hopeless," said John.

"I see," I said, "But it worked out."

He chuckled.

"Hopefully we won't have to stay here long," I said.

"Trust me," said John, "You think it is just a month or two, then it turns into a year. You might have to get comfortable if that happens… we'll set you up a proper bedroom."

"Well I certainly don't want to intrude on your honeymoon," I said.

John chuckled a little more, "Oh, that reminds me, I am part of a new farmers co-op. We are trying to use gene-modified crops and livestock but with an emphasis on owning all the material and crops ourselves rather than being dependent on a big company for supplies. If you are interested, we could use more people like you. We are trying to fill up a gene lab with as many brilliant biology people as we can, I am sure that they would be interested in someone like you."

"I will think about it," I said, "But I am a bit tired of being in the middle of nowhere, so I would prefer something more like a big city."

"The main lab is just outside Nashville," said John.

I blinked, "Ew, country music."

John nodded, "Fair."

I then got to exploring the house. The downstairs had a living room and a family room, a dining room, and a kitchen. The upstairs had two bedrooms, an office, a game room where I could set up my laptop, and a laundry room. The whole thing was well-lit, somewhat open floor plan, very warm colors, and nice and tidy. I was jealous of John and Trip living in such a nice house.

Eventually Trip got home and made dinner for everyone. He made a point of showing Mary how everything was vegan before he got started. He made false vegan fried chicken, soy milk instead of regular milk, vegan eggs, and plant-grown chicken breasts, with a side of mashed potatoes, corn on the cob, and a bowl of fruit. It was around this point that I got nervous about the prospect of gaining a few pounds if dinner was always going to be like this, and going to taste this good.

At the end of dinner, Mary spoke up, "I would like to thank Trip again, not only for making dinner, but also for showing me how everything was either vegan or false vegan. I honestly was expecting to have to make my own food, or to just get a salad if I was lucky. So the fact that you went above and beyond… I really appreciate it."

"It was the least I could do," said Trip.

"This is great," said John, "But now you are making me feel guilty for not saying thank you more often."

"Isn't our deal that I do the cooking and cleaning, and you bring the money home?" asked Trip.

"Yes but I still feel guilty."

We chatted after everything was put in the dishwasher.

I rested on the couch all night and slept well. I was pleasantly surprised by how comfortable it was.

In the morning I got a late start and Trip interrupted my search for cereal and coffee with bacon, eggs, and sausage, and also coffee that would make a barista blush. When John came down I had an important question.

"Are you trying to fatten me up? Cause at this rate it might happen." I then noticed that John was still very thin. "How are you not two hundred pounds at this point?"

John smiled, "Don't worry, Trip is good, but I get my exercise working the family business, also we have a small gym in the basement. Weights, treadmill, the whole deal."

I shuddered at the thought of exercise.

"If you want something less intense, Trip and I were going to go bird watching today, maybe it would be safe for you to come along."

The door-bell rang and John ran off to get it.

"Hello, Sue," said John.

"Yep," said Sue, as she stepped in and looked around, "Nice place you got here."

"Thanks," said John, "In all fairness it's my parent's place, but they just moved out and left it to me, like what dad is trying to do with the farm. The house kind of comes with it."

"How long ago did you parents move out?" asked Mary.

"A few months ago," said John, "But it doesn't feel real yet. I only started sleeping in the master bedroom because they converted my previous bedroom into a game room for me and my friends." He turned to Sue, "Anyways I was wondering if it would be OK to take Mary and Trixie out hiking and birdwatching some time. If they get cooped up or something."

"Depends," said Sue. "How good is your cellphone reception?"

"Surprisingly good," said John with a smile.

Sue nodded, "Should be OK then; our main safety feature is distance. So as long as you don't go too far."

"We will be careful," said John.

Sue nodded, "And give me a call if you do go out."

John nodded, then turned to me.

"You don't have to join us by the way. It's an option for when you fully get to know me and when you are extremely stir-crazy."

I nodded, "That makes sense."

"Anyway, Ms. Sue why are you here?" asked John.

"Just Sue," she said. "And I was checking in on everyone, making sure that this wasn't too much on anyone. Also hope you don't mind we did a quick background check on you."

"I thought I signed for that," said John.

"You did, and we found nothing concerning."

"Soooo?"

"Just wanted to let you know, and to say hi, and maybe give you an idea of what is going on."

"I will grab everyone and you can update us."

It was in that moment that Trip walked in.

"Is everything OK… oh hi Sue."

"Ah Trip, good, we can get started," said Sue.

John gestured for her to follow him and we gathered around the dining room table.

"So the short version is that Mr. Walker knows nothing," began Sue. "We tried interrogating him but after working with his lawyer, it is clear that he is an idiot. We have the number he got info on and it's Snow's number."

"So my idiot father used his regular cell phone to contact him?"

Sue nodded, "And he texted Jay the list of people he needed killed."

Trip shook his head, "My father always was stupid."

"Unfortunately you are also on his list," said Sue, looking directly at Trip.

"He wants me dead too," said Trip without even mild shock. "He always hated John, and that I didn't want to get involved in his shady business, and that I am gay, and that one time I tried being vegetarian. Oh and that I tried to find a way to go to college."

"I take it your relationship with your dad isn't great," said Mary.

Trip nodded, "He only liked me when I was a five-year-old that looked up to him. As I grew up, well, he grew hostile."

"Enough to want you dead?" asked Mary.

Trip nodded "I could see it."

Sue sighed, "If things get really hairy we can get witness protection involved. For now, I can offer it but if you feel safe enough here…"

"I never told Dad where I was going," said Trip. "He doesn't even know my old address. I haven't spoken to him or most of my family in months. So I doubt he knows anything."

Sue looked to Mary.

"Well, we are an hour's drive away from where we were," said Mary. "It's a bit of the middle of nowhere, so I don't feel in danger here."

Sue looked to me.

"I don't feel like I need full witness protection yet," I said. "If you recommended it I might change my mind but for now I don't want to turn my life upside down, again."

Sue nodded, "I am not going to push it for now." She began, "Just be careful, stay in a group and avoid dark alleys."

"So business as usual for young women," said Mary. "Got it."

"Right," said Sue. "Good." She turned to Trip and John, "Are you two going to be OK?"

"We are two gay men in a conservative area," said John. "We know when you need to run away."

"Good," said Sue. "Glad that the worst aspects of society have prepared the four of you for someone wanting to hurt you. Now that I feel incredibly depressed and am wondering how we are going to fix our broken society, I will leave the four of you alone and hope that you can keep each other safe. Now if you excuse me, I have to go be depressed for an hour then give myself a pep talk and remind myself why I became a lawyer in the first place."

"Why did you become a lawyer in the first place?" asked John.

"The money obviously," said Sue, "If I keep this up, I can retire in negative five years." She then stood up and left.

"If she can retire five years ago why is she still working now?" asked Mary to me.

"Good question," shouted Sue from the door. "Let me know when you have an answer because I sure don't."

We heard the door close on her way out.

"So when you guys inevitably get house sick I was thinking we could go for a local hike," said Trip. "My future father-in-law introduced me to it, got me back into the outdoors. It might be nice on a sunny day to avoid cabin fever."

"Hold on," said Mary. "Don't you two have a wedding to be planning?"

"How do you know about that," said John. "I mean you're right but…"

"Trixie told me on the way up," said Mary.

"Sorry," I said.

John looked at us with mock anger, shaking his fist with all the energy of a particularly lazy sloth.

Trip cleared his throat, "In all seriousness, the plan is for a short trip to the nearest justice of the peace, and then a small reception with select friends and family at home, on a date that will be easy to remember."

Mary frowned, "The first gay wedding I might be invited to, and it's just a trip to the justice of the piece."

"Blame my big sister," said John, "She had the big wedding, and seeing her and her husband nearly call off the wedding and separate over planning it turned us off of a big wedding."

It took three whole days for the four of us to become stir-crazy. The sun was shining, hardly a cloud in the sky, a day after a downpour. John's helpers got everything done in the morning. And it was not as hot as it could have been. So we decided it was a good day for a hike.

At first it was going well enough. John identified several species of bird. He took us on a big loop. Then Trip found hoof prints.

"I think I can track it," he said, "We might go bushwhacking a bit, but we could see some deer, we might get close if we are quiet."

"Sure," I said.

Mary nodded and then John turned to Trip, "After you," he said.

We then followed Trip along the tracks, and found at the end of it a sheep, a Sapi sheep... we had stumbled on one of the sheep.

"Is that...?" whispered John.

"One of my father's sheep," whispered Trip, "Yes."

"Maybe it will recognize me," I said, "Let me try something."

I stood up. "Hey," I said to the sheep. "Ok, so maybe straw is cheaper and the grass is free, and as I am learning, hay is more bedding than food but nonetheless hello."

The sheep looked at me. If ever there was a sheep with an unamused look this was the sheep.

"And now that I have your attention, my friends and I were going on a hike and sort of stumbled on you, but my old grad school advisor can change you back to human. If you wait here we can call her in, get you back to normal."

The sheep shook its head.

"Do you want to stay a sheep?" I asked.

The sheep shook its head again, then walked up to me, then past me to Trip, John, and Mary. Then the sheep baaed at them.

"I have Lou on the phone," said Trip, "He and the rest of them are on the way. But it's going to take a while for them to get here.

The sheep nodded and then sat down.

I rejoined the group and we began the process of waiting around. By the time Lou, Sick, Sue and everyone else had gotten here, Trip had trekked back home, come back with a water bowl for the sheep, some fresh grass clippings which the Sapi sheep ate up, and a Monopolizing board. We managed to get halfway through the game while waiting for them.

"Seriously?" said Sick.

"Well you took your sweet time," said Trip.

The sheep baaed.

"Yeah these guys are OK," I said to the sheep.

"How did you know that was what… they were saying?" said Lou.

"I didn't," I said, "I just guessed."

The sheep baaed, got up, started walking for a few feet, then turned around to look at us.

"After you," said Mary to the sheep.

The sheep started walking again and after Lou and Sick shrugged at each other, we followed. Trip packed up the Monopolizing game quickly and caught up. The sheep would stop every few yards, look back at us, and then start again.

After half an hour the sheep looked at us one last time, stopped, sat down, and looked at something. An edge of a thicket, thorny bushes, and all that. Beyond it, peering through a thick area of forest, just barely visible, was a house. Listening carefully, we could hear baaing.

Lou looked to the sheep and whispered, "Is this where Snow lives?"

The sheep blinked.

"The guy who turns people into sheep," I whispered, "That's what he means."

The sheep nodded.

"Can you take us to a place where we can see the pens?" whispered Sick.

The sheep nodded and led us to another area. There was a particularly filthy pen with a bunch of Sapi sheep in it surrounded by rickety fencing, nearby was a pile of bones, with what looked like sheep skulls in it.

"Ok. Why are there sheep bones?" I asked at a whisper.

"Don't know," said Sick, "And I don't know if I want to find out."

"We can get GPS coordinates on our cell phones," said Sick, "Come back with a force and a warrant. We will rescue the rest of the sheep, find out if the sheep skulls are from where I hope they aren't, and then bag and tag everything and go home." He turned to the sheep, "For now we will get you back to human, then we will rescue the rest, I am assuming that's why you brought us here."

The sheep nodded.

"We will rescue them, I am sorry that it will take more time after taking so long, but we will do it right, and we will ensure that Snow receives justice."

Then we heard the screech of a car.

"Down," whispered Mary.

We kept our heads down, so did the sheep, and listened. Then I heard loud knocking.

"Open up Snow," shouted a voice that sounded exactly like Dick from B.O.O.B.

"You got a warrant?" said Snow's voice.

I peeked up just enough to see what was going on. I saw a flash then I heard a gunshot.

"Get out or I will kill them," shouted Snow.

CHAPTER 21

"What do we do now?" I asked Sick at a whisper.

"You stay here, no, take our Sapi friend back to where you were, get them to your house or something," said Sick.

"What about you?" asked Trip.

"We will catch up," said Lou.

"I think I can get us back," said Trip.

"Go," said Lou.

And we left, or at least we tried, but everyone panicked maybe 100 feet out when we heard a whole lot of shots. So we ran, and in running, got separated. So plan B, I found a place to hide in, then started figuring out how I would get out of this mess. I could probably use my phone to either call Trip and ask for help from him, or just use the GPS feature to navigate to his house. The latter would be possible as I already have his new address as I used my phone to navigate here in the first place. If that didn't work, so long as I saved some of my battery I could still call for help and wait for rescue.

"AH HA," shouted Snow who suddenly appeared right next to me. "WHAT AREN'T YOU… WELL YOU WILL MAKE A GOOD HOSTAGE."

He pointed a gun at me, looked like an old west style revolver, and grabbed my shoulder.

"STAND UP," he shouted right next to my ear. I didn't argue, I just stood up.

Then I had a brain wave. "You don't need to shout," I said as loudly as I felt I could.

"BE QUIET," shouted Snow.

"Why?" I asked loudly.

"BECAUSE I SAID SO," shouted Snow. "NOW MOVE," he said, pulling on me.

"What are you afraid of? No one would hear me shout for help," I said again loudly, trying to walk the way he wanted me to walk.

"JUST SHUT UP," shouted Snow. "I'LL KILL YOU."

I decided not to push my luck for now and let him push me in the direction he wanted to go. We rounded a tree and ran into Sick pointing a pistol in our general direction.

"Let her go Snow," said Sick.

"PUT THE GUN DOWN, I'LL KILL HER," shouted Snow.

Sick did nothing, just standing there, keeping the pistol pointed in our direction.

"I SAID PUT IT DOWN," growled Snow.

I had another brain wave. "Why would he do that?" I asked.

"BECAUSE I WILL KILL YOU IF HE DOESN'T," said Snow in my ear loudly enough I am sure Sick heard. "YOU WANT TO LIVE, RIGHT? SO WHY DON'T YOU TELL THE NICE POLICE OFFICER TO. DO. AS. I. SAY?"

"If you kill me, you're next," I said.

I could feel Snow suddenly become rigid, "WHAT?" he asked.

"You shoot me, I die, and suddenly you no longer have a hostage." I began, "There is a man with a gun, in a policeman's uniform with a pistol already pointed at you, what do you think will happen before my body hits the ground?"

Suddenly Snow began to hyperventilate. He was starting to panic, hopefully that would mean he would make some sort of mistake other than killing me.

"THEN… WE ARE AT AN IMPASSE," he began.

Sick seemed to subtly point his gun more to my right than at us.

" I CAN'T KILL HER BUT YOU CAN'T RISK SHOOTING," said Snow. "OTHERWISE YOU MIGHT HIT HER. WE SHOULD TALK."

"So that the next guy with a bright idea to take a hostage can look at this and think it worked," said Sick. "No, we don't have anything to talk about."

"BUT I WILL KILL HER," said Snow, tightening his hold on me.

"You're a bit of a one-trick pony," I said hoping my terror wasn't getting through. "Even I am getting tired of hearing this bluff."

"Besides," said Lou from behind me to my left. "You are more outnumbered here than you thought."

Now Snow really began to hyperventilate. I got the sense, based on what I was feeling behind me, that he was looking back and forth. "WHAT? HOW?"

"I'm sneaky," said Lou. "Now you have ten seconds to let her go before I blast your brains out."

A second later I felt a push that nearly resulted in me falling down on my face. I caught myself and took a few steps forward, turned around, and saw Lou arresting Snow.

"You have the right to remain silent," began Lou.

"Are you alright?" asked Sick.

I took a moment to collect myself, "I need a change of underwear, and probably also my pants, but other than that I'm OK."

"Right," said Sick, "I've got to help Lou, then we will get you out of here. Maybe call Trip and let him know that everything is OK now."

Sick then went over to where Lou was reading Snow his rights and got his phone out.

"So you know that tip we got," began Sick into the phone.

Half an hour later, other officers showed up; one of them took me back to John's place, where I changed, took a shower, and after looking up online what to do with soiled underwear, got laundry started.

Then I drove back to the area so that I could pick up John, Mary, and Trip. When I got back the area at Snow's backup house was quite busy. There was a swarm of police cars, an ambulance and several non-police cars. Sue had arrived and flagged me down shortly after I showed up.

"Feel better?" she asked.

"Cleaner," I said. "How is the mess here?"

"Messy," said Sue. "Turns out Jay bought this house for Snow with Snow's money."

"That how Dick from B.O.O.B. got here?" I aside.

Sue nodded, "We had the same idea in our investigation of course, and were close to having a warrant to go in anyway."

"Is this a problem?" I asked.

"Dick's involvement will give Snow's lawyer a shred of an argument," said Sue. "Should Snow have taken a hostage and shot a federal agent, no, but the fact that Dick was trying to enter without a warrant says something. They will have a real argument to make in court that this was done improperly. I don't think it will be enough to make a huge difference but still…"

"Well at least no one got shot."

"Actually Dick did," said Sue with a smile. "A good sign for our case."

I nodded, "The sheep bones?"

"We aren't sure they are sheep bones yet," said Sue. "But we are missing seven sheep, and there are seven skulls in the pile, a few lamb chops in the fridge, and the forensics guy says it looks like someone cut meat from the bones." Sue grimaced, "It's too early to say for sure but… I will keep you informed."

I nodded, "Will we need me to help get them back to human?" I asked.

"I doubt it," said Sue. "We had you and Calamity make extra solution so we probably don't need any more."

I then saw an unmarked black sedan pull up and park in part of the mess of cars that Hank had joined. And Gerald Mann, from Marks Jewels stepped out, along with two burly men in suits.

He walked in our general direction, nodded to Sue and I, and then kept walking toward an ambulance that had parked in the mess of cars.

It was at this point that I finally noticed that Dick, from B.O.O.B., was already sitting on the edge of the ambulance back. He had a bunch of bandages on his left leg.

I was too curious to not get closer to see what was going on.

"Well, well, well," said Mann, "If it isn't the problem child."

"Hey," said Dick. "I was trying to do something rather than sitting around doing nothing like most of the people at the office."

"If you had done nothing, then you would have done more," said Mann. "You were stretching the limits of our jurisdiction, not even trying to work with local law enforcement, tried to go into a citizen's house without even trying to get a warrant, and got shot for your troubles." Mann sighed, "You were only saved because local officers and a few civilians working with them happened to be in the area when you got shot in the leg. As one of their lawyers kindly informed me on the way in, they had already made the same connection you did. And again the civilians working with the local police stumbled on this anyway. If you had not arrived here at all, then after finding this place and informing local police, they would have gotten a warrant and likely arrested Snow in a day or two. As it is, someone got taken hostage for a minute, and your involvement made everything messier."

Dick scoffed, "What was I supposed to do, stay in the office and look at paperwork?"

Mann nodded, "If you had, you might have noticed who was stealing the bug weed, you know, the one thing we were supposed to actually monitor. Allowing for some to be stolen right from under our noses and some civilian and other enforcement agencies to find it."

"Oh you mean her?" said Dick, looking at me. "She is just an idiot and a woman, she doesn't know anything."

"And yet she found what you didn't," said Mann. "She did more for this agency than you ever did, and her results actually meant something." He sighed, "The one good thing that came from this, is that it was so embarrassing that Congress decided that we needed some reforms for the Bureau Of Odd Biology."

"How is that good?" said Dick.

"Because I can now fire you," said Mann.

"You can't do that," said Dick.

"You're partly right," said Mann. "Your uncle makes you un-fireable, but I can transfer you to our new office in South Carolina."

Dick suddenly gulped.

"You… can't be serious."

Mann smiled an evil grin, "I am very serious. Are you ready to move to South Carolina?"

"Please…not there." Dick quivered, "Is… there anywhere else? Somewhere that has… roads that aren't terrible and… ok traffic."

Mann shook his head with a smile.

Dick took a deep breath, "My resignation will be on your desk before you get back."

"My flight home is in three hours," said Mann. "So you better hurry."

Dick grabbed a pair of crutches and moved off to one car, got in and drove off.

Mann walked up to me, "You know if you're in the job market, there is a new government agency looking for workers."

I looked at him.

Mann sighed, "They are calling it the Office Monitoring Gene-mods, O.M.G for short."

I shook my head, "Seriously that is almost as bad as the Bureau Of Odd Biology."

"At least it no longer implies human anatomy," said Mann.

"Or that the agency is an idiot," I said, "Or a bird."

Mann chuckled, "Still, if you need a job I am sure you would be a shoo-in. If nothing else your thesis interests me.

You tried to grow bug weed, and while you didn't succeed given everything else you have seen you might fit right in with the agency I am trying to build." He turned to Sue, "Also I will need a lawyer to help get the agency's founding documents drawn up. If your private practice is getting tiring, we could offer fewer working hours… for more pay."

"Why me specifically?" asked Sue.

"Because you now have some idea of what we are doing," said Mann. "Do you know how many lawyers have any idea of what we are doing?"

Sue shook her head.

"Not many, said Mann. "And most of them work for Windbreakers, so I might as well try to get the only exception working for me." He smiled, "And helping decide what the laws will be?"

"Are you trying to appeal to my sense of ambition?" asked Sue.

"Is it working?" said Mann.

Sue was silent for a moment, then she looked down.

"Yes," said Sue.

Mann chuckled to himself, "If either of you are interested give me a call." He handed us business cards and walked away.

I looked to Sue, "What happens now?"

"Well either the long boring part begins as we set up a case or they realize that they have none and give up. Either way, it won't be interesting so I will let you know if we need you, otherwise I would take some time off."

I nodded and called Mom to let her know that I was in fact down for a cruise in two weeks with the rest of the family and not to give my ticket away after all.